The Way Up

To Sheri,
Thank you for being so cool! :)
Enjoy!

9/30/2018

PROVERBS 16:9

Jose Angel Rodriguez

José Angel Rodriguez

Carpenter's Son Publishing

The Way Up

©2018 by Jose Angel Rodriguez

All rights reserved. No part of this book may be reproduced or transmitted in any form or by any means, electronic or mechanical, including photocopying, recording, or by any information storage and retrieval system, without permission in writing from the copyright owner.

Published by Carpenter's Son Publishing, Franklin, Tennessee

Published in association with Larry Carpenter of Christian Book Services, LLC
www.christianbookservices.com

Scripture taken from THE HOLY BIBLE, NEW INTERNATIONAL VERSION®, NIV® Copyright © 1973, 1978, 1984, 2011 by Biblica, Inc.™ Used by permission. All rights reserved worldwide.

Edited by Robert Irvin

Cover and Interior Design by Suzanne Lawing

Printed in the United States of America

978-1-946889-39-3

CONTENTS

Paying the Piper	5
Father and Son	13
Making Plans	25
Susan	37
Detroit at Last	45
Life Paths	59
Ripples	73
Light Probes Darkness	79
Willy	93
Bobby Makes His Move	109
A Better Deal	125
Light Breaks Through	137
The U-Turn	151
No Greater Love	169

DEDICATION

To Jesus Christ, who changed my life.

To my wife, Sandy, who overlooks my failings and is the greatest encourager this side of Heaven.

To the many people, starting with my parents, who invested in me and believed in me when I had my doubts.

The adventure continues.

ONE

Paying the Piper

They were cursing at him and laughing at the same time. Jack was outnumbered, and he had been outfought for some time. Now it was just a matter of time as they took out their anger on him.

Nighttime in an abandoned warehouse makes for a convenient time and place to execute revenge. Throw in alcohol and drugs, and the effect is like pouring gasoline on a fire. The thugs beating on him didn't care who heard them, and certainly if anyone saw them, no one would dare try to intervene. Jack's own cries and groans joined their jeers in a cacophony acknowledging the steps on this dance to death . . .

This frenzied scene began earlier in the evening. When you live in the shadows of the underworld, paranoia is a virtue. And it's been said by more than one person that it's not paranoia if they really are out to get you. Jack had enemies, which he had made the old-fashioned way. He worked at it, and apparently was quite successful. As the evening played out, Jack stored up an ironically humorous and dark thought: *Note to self: Do not steal another man's drugs, money, or woman.* Any one of these can, and will, result in a strain on relationships. And, ultimately, to the predicament Jack found himself in later that night.

Whoever said that what the world needs now is love wasn't thinking of loving money. Someone else said that the love of money is the root of all evil. Certainly, someone loved their money enough to kill Jack for it. Jack didn't get it: the news media is replete with stories of business bigwigs who do not hesitate to skim a little money off the top of their profits for themselves. Sure, some get caught, but they don't get the death penalty. At most, they spend a little time in jail, but most just pay a fine and get back to business as usual.

Simply put, Jack had misjudged Jason. The two of them went back quite a ways. Jack first met Jason when he was released from prison and needed a place to stay. Jason stayed with Jack for a short while until he decided to move in with a girl he met through the prisoner letter-writing program. But Jason and the woman had trouble from the start, and Jack needed a roommate to help him with expenses, so Jack took a chance and brought Jason back in. It wasn't long before Jack realized that Jason's time in prison served to help Jason hone his criminal skills. He was a large man—at least larger than Jack. Not in an intimidating way, but more so in a way that spoke of self-confidence. It wasn't until later that Jack learned that this apparent self-assurance was actually a façade for an insecure and angry personality that hid unresolved issues. The fact that Jason was also quite charismatic sucked Jack in to believing that they could have a profitable relationship. Jason *knew* people. People looked up to him, and everything he touched seemed to turn to gold. Jack could learn a lot from him—and he did.

It wasn't long before they were controlling much of the drug trade in their area. They developed a network of dealers and mules that ensured they bought the drugs cheap and sold them at a nice profit. The best part was that very few in the network knew of Jason and Jack. They were what is called, in the trade, ghost owners. And, essentially, partners. Money was sent to numbered accounts in Switzerland, and shell companies were used to make sure nothing could be traced back to the two.

This was profitable for both of them—until greed raised its ugly head. They began noticing some of the downrange leadership wanted more of the action. These men were not satisfied with what they had. In fact, they forgot that they had nothing when they came to work for Jason. The more money they made, the more they wanted. It became a vicious circle of hunger for money and power. Eventually, Jason's insecurities surfaced. He reached the point in which he didn't trust anyone, including Jack.

Jack couldn't claim that he was entirely innocent. He had begun to skim a little of the profits. He reasoned that he could set aside enough so that at some point he could go out on his own. Jason's paranoia had begun to affect their relationship, and Jason was no longer the golden boy that Jack once thought.

If it is argued that it's a dog-eat-dog world in regular business, then it is doubly so in the criminal world. When someone says they have your back, the first thought that comes to mind is they are about to stab you in the back. No one trusts anyone, and there are always those trying to get to the top of the mountain in any way they can, but without the inconvenience of having to abide by any rules. That is not to say that there is no law. It is an *unspoken* law. But even if unspoken, justice is swiftly meted out. It may be unevenly applied, but the same could be said for a legal system that incarcerates many people for small crimes and lets out moneyed people with a slap on the wrist.

You don't know what you don't know, and what Jack didn't know was that Jason had placed one of his bought-and-paid-for accountants to follow Jack's part of the money trail. It wasn't long before Jack noticed that a wall was building between Jason and himself. Jason was not as friendly; they no longer laughed at those who were awkwardly trying to outflank them in the business. Jason's countenance became more serious and untrusting. This totally caught Jack by surprise.

*****

Jack had just arrived back at his apartment after spending most of the evening at the hospital with a friend of his, Kathy, and her family. Her brother, Will, had gotten beat up a few weeks back, and had been in a coma—until tonight. What he witnessed in the hospital that night was impossible as far as he was concerned. He would try to wrap his head around it later.

After leaving the hospital, Jack went to one of his favorite watering spots. It was close to his apartment so he could walk home in case he drank too much. Tonight was one of those nights. So here it was, after

10 p.m., Jack had just got home, and Jason was on the phone, wanting him to go to a warehouse on the other side of town. In his inebriated state of mind, Jack tried to convince Jason to put this off until morning.

"Man, can't this wait?"

"This is a big one. I'm not sure the numbers are right, and I don't want to mess it up." He was referring to a shipment that was due soon.

"Well, I can tell that you've been drinking, and I know I've been drinking. It seems to me that we would be better off waiting until tomorrow when our heads are a little clearer."

"That's why I asked Bobby to meet us there," Jason quickly answered. "He hasn't been drinking, and he is the best numbers guy after us in the organization. Come on. It won't take long, and you'll be back in your comfy bed before you know it."

Bobby was an accountant in his own right, and Jack later found out that he was the one who tracked his numbers and gave him up. The halo didn't quite fit Bobby, though. All he wanted was to get higher in the business, and the only way to do that was to knock Jack down. Jack hated hypocrites.

He also hated surprises. Too many surprises in his life had been bad ones. This was no different.

When he got to the warehouse, it wasn't just Bobby and Jason who were there. He should have known right away that things were not right. When you see four big "uninvited" men at a secret meeting late at night, your antennae should go up; bells should go off in your head. It wasn't long before Jack realized he was the object of this meeting. Jason spoke first.

"J, how long have we known each other?"

"A long time, Jason. Three, four years. What is this all about?"

"You know, you think you know someone, you trust them. You let your guard down, and inevitably, they let you down."

"What are you talking about? Why are these guys here?"

"Do you remember Mikey?" Jason went on, ignoring Jack's question. "Remember when he tried to peel away a part of our business? He wasn't satisfied that we had set him up to be more successful than he had ever been before in life. Remember his reaction when we called him on it?" Jason was staring off into space, a slight smile betraying his enjoyment of not only the remembrance of Mikey, but also what was about to take place.

Jason, who had been Jack's friend and business partner for these several years, was now accusing him of stepping out of bounds. "We had an understanding," Jason said. "We didn't even have anything in writing to cement our relationship because we were men of honor, of integrity. Our word was our bond. It should have been enough." This would have been humorous if not for the seriousness of the matter at hand. One thing Jack had learned for sure: it is true that there is no honor among thieves. Maybe Jason had fooled himself, but Jack never truly trusted him. Life had taught Jack that you had to watch out for number one, and that was yourself first and foremost. It was only a matter of time before they would tire of each other. All relationships come to an end, either by a parting of ways or by death. He was unsure as to how this one would end.

Jack stood there listening to Bobby recite alleged infractions that he had committed with the money that was supposed to be evenly shared with Jason. Although some were true, it didn't really matter that any of them had extenuating circumstances that might have justified his actions. In Jason's eyes, Jack had stolen money that was rightfully his, and that was an unforgivable sin. He just wanted Jack to admit being a crook.

"J, what do you think we should do about this? After all, you and I started this together. You were like a brother to me. You took me in when nobody else would give me the time of day."

Jason's phone rang. It was both an interruption and a distraction. Jason was not pleased. Jack knew him long enough to see that his short fuse was getting shorter as he listened to the voice on the other end: Margaret.

Margaret was the woman who met Jason through writing letters to prisoners. She was the only one to meet him when he got out. With the fifty dollars the state gave him, and the one change of clothes that he had, Jason was lucky to have her around. He needed her more than she needed him at the time. He immediately moved in with her, but corresponding with letters is not the same as living with someone. It wasn't long before they realized that their relationship was not exactly made in Heaven. Jason wanted to leave, and she was anxious for him to leave.

But like moths to a flame, they never totally broke it off. They lived together off and on, and now they were back on—somewhat. Jason split his time between his place with Jack and staying with Margaret. For all his bravado, Jason was a needy person, and Margaret had a need to rescue people. She enabled him in his insecurities, and he affirmed her need to be needed. It was a mutually destructive arrangement. The fact that she was calling him in the middle of the night did not sit well with Jason. It showed her concern for his well-being, but to Jason, it also smacked of her attempt to keep him on a tight leash. Nobody was going to tell him what to do, and they would do well not to try to hold him accountable. Margaret had messed up on both counts.

"Maggie!" Jack's suspicions were right. Jason never called her Maggie—unless he wanted to insult her. She had picked up that moniker early in life. It was originally intended as a term of endearment. Everyone called her Maggie—until kids learned they could hurt her feelings by calling her Maggie the maggot. Children can be so cruel. Some say it's because of the base nature of humans. You never hear of children coming up with names or descriptive phrases that lift up others. It's like the proverbial pecking order. Chickens are known to peck on the weaker members of a group until they destroy them. People don't seem to be much different, Jack often thought. Anyway, Jason was mad at being interrupted, and Jack was sure Margaret was rethinking her decision to call him.

"I told you that I would be home when I get home! I don't care what time it is, and you shouldn't either. Go to bed. I don't need you checking up on me!" He was trying to rein himself in, but you could tell from the way Jason rolled his eyes that this was not going to end well. He didn't even hang up. The next thing Jack saw was Jason hurling the phone against the wall and small pieces of plastic and glass flying everywhere.

Jason didn't cuss. He just never did. He would break things, he would yell, he would punch the wall. But he never used any harder language than an occasional "darn it." He did all four of those things this time. It was like he forgot anyone else was in the room. Jack thought he might just forget about him. But Jack was wrong.

At some point in his rampage, he turned his wrath to Jack. "That's why I don't trust anyone! They always try to take advantage of my good graces. And *you* . . . you haven't been any better. You are the Judas of my life. I trusted you with the money, and you let me down. I turn my back, and you conspire against me. What excuse do you have, you worthless piece of junk? Were you going to give it to the Jack retirement charity? Maybe you were going to invest it in the stock market and make a killing for us? You are a piece of work. I can't believe I didn't see through you before." Putting his face right up to Jack's, he snarled, "You really give me no choice."

Bobby had done his job well. He had spent months convincing Jason that Jack was not to be trusted, that he had embezzled money, that it was only a matter of time before he would try to remove Jason. Only part of that was true, but it was obvious Jack would get no chance to explain anything. The slim possibility of that happening dropped to none when Margaret's phone call pushed Jason over the edge. Turning to the other men in the room, Jason said, "Get him out of here."

Jack had to try. "Jason, you don't know what you're doing. Bobby is the one who is setting you up. You and I have been together for . . . . " He had no chance to finish before a fist smashed into his face. It was a searing, jolting pain, and Jack felt fairly certain a bone in his face had just been broken.

"Shut up." It was Steve. He never liked Jack, and Jack could see the satisfaction on his face from finally getting a chance to get him. And it seemed that this was the needed cue for the other three guys to take their turns. One after the other, while two held him up, one would pummel him. It wasn't long before Jack could see blood on their knuckles, and it wasn't theirs. Jack didn't really need to see it, because he could taste it. And these guys seemed to relish giving him the beating of his life.

"I said, get him out of here! You're messing up the place! I don't need to see this," Jason yelled. He had a strange set of values. He detested betrayal, but he didn't see that Bobby was betraying Jack— and would eventually betray him. He didn't like violence, but the only issue he had with Jack's being beaten in his presence was that his space was getting messy with Jack's blood and spittle. Jason's sense of justice revolved around him getting his way. His friendship was conditioned on what he got from the other person. If Jason thought you were using him, he could not see that he did the same to others.

This had never happened before, not that Jack had witnessed. Sure, there were people who disappeared, but Jason always had a reason why "they are no longer with us." It usually had something to do with them needing to move from the area, or they had gotten sick. In Jack's wanting to believe Jason, he never really questioned his business friend on these types of matters. Deep down, Jack wanted to accept the oft-spoken philosophy that people are basically good. His life had been hard since he left home, but he had never experienced total darkness of the heart lived out in someone else—especially someone he had come to trust and believe in.

Jack was dragged outside into an alley, where the beating continued. There was enough light that he could see near glee and giddiness mixed with hatred on the faces of the men doing the beating. It was as if they were born for this. It was like a demonic force was goading them to make the beating worse. When they saw his pain, and heard the sounds of the beating upon Jack's body, they reacted as if fuel had been added to a fire. They could not get enough.

The pain. Jack did not know that a human body could experience such excruciating pain. They wouldn't stop. After being knocked down, someone kicked him in the stomach, which was followed by blows to the head and chest. It was hard to catch his breath, much less fight back . . .

It looked like this was going to be the end of the road. Someone once told Jack that your life is the result of the many decisions you make. As he slipped into unconsciousness, the decisions that got him to this place replayed themselves before his mind's eye.

TWO

Father and Son

You don't know what you don't know. Until something happens that brings the reality of your ignorance to the forefront of your mind.

Jack grew up in a solid family. Of course, he thought everyone had the same kind of family he had. His father owned his own business. He came home every evening, and to Jack's knowledge, always loved Jack's mother. Jack's mom was one of those stay-at-home mothers. She made the house a home, his father used to say. They ate together around the kitchen table every evening, and sometimes Dad would even come home for lunch. Jack didn't ever remember going hungry. All his friends had similar families. Divorce was rare and frowned upon, and a two-car family—like Jack's—was seen by many as a rich one.

That's just the way life was. But a child growing up eventually begins to notice things when things don't seem right. Having a limited understanding, it wasn't long before this little boy, Jack, developed an attitude that life was not fair. Particularly grating was the perception that his parents were unduly strict, which served to limit his creative juices. What kind of parents make their children come in the house when the streetlights come on in the evening? What kind of parents restrict a child's television viewing time during the time the TV industry says is "family time"? And why was it called family time, Jack wondered, if it wasn't intended for the whole family? Jack's dad and mom were the kind of parents who didn't lend much weight to what other kids' parents let their sons and daughters do.

So while other kids were staying out late at night, Jack was under a curfew that had him home during the most fun parts of the evening.

It got worse when Jack got old enough to get a driver's license. His father took his sweet time teaching him how to drive. They had driver's training at school, but Jack's father believed he had to teach Jack "the right way" before he could take on the state test. Something about the school not being responsible for Jack; instead, as father, he was. Jack was six months past his sixteenth birthday before he finally got his license. Of course, he had to endure the interminable learner's permit period, when he couldn't drive without an adult in the car. He felt all these restrictions certainly limited his ability to impress girls—and anyone else to whom he could show off his new driving skills.

Jack thought getting his driver's license would finally result in the freedom he deserved, but he was once again sadly mistaken. His father had rules. *Why is it that every time I earn a little more freedom, rules come attached?* Jack would ask himself. "Rules are for your benefit," his father would say. *Yeah, right,* Jack thought.

"Bring the car back with the same amount of gas you had when you began," his father would say. Begging, borrowing, or stealing the money was not a good option, so Jack would have to give up some of his free time to earn enough money to put gas in the car. As an added treat, Jack's father would always check the odometer to make sure Jack hadn't strayed too far from home. "If his car was so important to him," Jack reasoned, "why doesn't he just buy one for me?" Problem solved, in Jack's book.

"When you leave one of your friends' houses to go to another, call us when you get there." This was before the advent of cell phones. Jack couldn't believe what he was hearing. *Are you kidding me?* he would think. His dad said something about being able to get in touch with him in case of an emergency. Jack suspected it was something else. *I'm not stupid,* Jack would tell himself.

"You may ask to use the car only on weekends, and only if I don't have plans already." Jack could see his social life evaporating like water after a light rain. He was beginning to see that his new driver's license was only coming in handy when his parents wanted him to pick up something at the store or chauffeur his younger brother or sister somewhere. That's it: he was an unpaid, on-call chauffeur.

"The speed limit sign is not a temperature sign. Obey it or walk." "With greater freedom comes greater responsibilities." On and on the rules went. He wanted to tell his father to take a chill pill, but he had been raised to respect his elders.

There were other stupid rules. Like the one about not calling or receiving calls after 9 p.m. during the week. Why? Because people, including his father, had to go to work the next day, and they were usually getting ready for bed by then. Jack wasn't against rules; he just felt they shouldn't infringe on his being able to make his own decisions.

Through the years, Jack's time at home became more and more unbearable. He convinced himself he had an unreasonable father, and a mother who would not stand up for him. Stifling limitations on his freedom kept him from developing socially. He imagined that the other kids at school were starting to look at him as some kind of pansy, and that resulted in the occasional fight, the lowering of his grades, and a restlessness that would not be tamed. While his friends were busy exploring what the world had to offer, Jack had to contend with curfews and work and chores and studies and responsibilities, none of which his peer group had—or so it appeared to Jack. He was told that he had all the freedom he wanted within the limits that everyone had to live under. His father tried to illustrate this by telling him that every game has its rules, and that life is, in a sense, a game. It needed rules, and it was the parents' responsibility to set rules that would help their children grow up to be productive citizens of society. When things got testy, which happened more than once, his father would say, "My house, my rules."

By the time Jack got close to his eighteenth birthday, he could hardly wait to leave the confinement of his parents' house. The fun times he had growing up as a child had long been forgotten by the perceived unfairness of his existence during his teen years. If "life is not fair," as his father used to say, then Jack was sure life with his father was the most unfair of all.

Mom and Dad had saved up money over the years to help Jack and his brother and sister pay for college. There was no guarantee any of them would attend college, but there was an unspoken expectation. After all, their parents wanted Jack, Don, and Becky to have the same or greater opportunities to be successful as they had. Jack's dad had paid attention to his father, and he'd taken advantage of opportunities that came his way to get ahead. Jack's father said that he liked to listen to the older guys around him. He used to say that there was great wisdom in what they said, and if you paid attention, you could learn a thing or two that would help you have it a little easier down the road. Jack's father studied people. He would say that he would rather learn from the mistakes of others than make them himself. He figured he would make enough of his own, so there was really no need to pile on by redoing the errors of others.

As the oldest, it was expected that Jack would set the example, that he would lead the way of maturity and responsibility by going to a good college, preferably close to home. Maybe within four or five years he would be well on the way to a nice life with a wife and kids (Mom wanted grandkids in the worst way), plus a nice job. But all that was the furthest thing from Jack's mind.

What Jack wanted was out. He wanted to get as far away as possible from his family and its crazy ways. He had read about some kids divorcing their parents—Jack actually looked into it—but it didn't look like such a move would work for him. He did learn one piece of helpful information along the way. The money that his parents scrimped and saved to send Jack and his siblings to college was not in a restricted account. It didn't have to be spent on college. His parents could withdraw it anytime and use it for whatever they wanted. Jack didn't know why they did it that way, because Dad was usually very meticulous about where he put his money. In any case, it presented an opportunity that Jack fully intended to take advantage of.

They might have known that he was up to something because, as usual, when he wanted something, Jack became unusually friendly and courteous. He washed and waxed the car. He mowed and trimmed the yard. One thing he had learned: before asking for something important, take steps to soften up the parents. One evening around the dinner table, Jack was sure his opportunity was suddenly in front of him.

"Dad, I have a question for you."

"Yes, son? What wisdom would you like me to lay on you tonight?" Jack's father always tried to use humor when he talked with his eldest son. He had high hopes for him, but it had become pretty obvious to Jack these past few years that they would not be agreeing on what that would look like. Jack had to hand it to his dad. The man just did not give up. *Maybe that is where I got my stubborn streak,* Jack thought. But back to the conversation: Mom sat there, just picking at her food, trying not to look concerned. Jack knew her well enough to know she was hanging on every word being spoken. She would only speak when she felt she would get the greatest impact from her words. As her firstborn, she lavished attention on Jack through his early years, but at around age twelve, she and Dad decided the father should play a greater role in Jack's upbringing. She had read somewhere that a father's influence was very important in the raising of children, especially sons. Other cultures even had ceremonies to mark the entrance of a young boy into adulthood, and these usually meant that he would fall more and more under the influence and tutelage of the dominant male in the family. That almost always meant the father.

Jack's younger brother, Don, and baby sister, Becky, also sat in silence, listening. Their lives had been made easier by learning what to say and do—and what *not* to say and do—through watching Jack.

"Dad, I've been thinking about my future."

"So have we," his father interjected.

"So, I've been thinking . . . I'm going to be eighteen this year, and I think it will be time for me to go out on my own."

"Really? What makes you think you're ready to do that?"

"Well, I thought about you and grandpa. Grandpa left home when he was fourteen. I know that was a different era, and there were different circumstances, but you yourself left when you finished high school at seventeen."

"That's right, but your grandfather was kicked out of the house after fighting with his father. I left home to join the Army. Is that what you want to do, join the Army?"

"I thought about it, and I may still join the reserves, but that's not really what I had in mind," Jack said, starting again. "I have a friend from school who has a job lined up in Detroit, and he said I could join him. We could share an apartment and split costs down the middle."

Detroit. You could see Jack's father's mind digesting this information and trying to come up with a response worthy of his intellect, one that could cross the barrier of Jack's know-it-all attitude. Mom was not so calculating. She was worried, and it showed. She had immediately calculated that Detroit was at least one overnight trip away.

Plains, Georgia was a sleepy little Southern town, with its expected charm and shortcomings. Located in some of the best farming country in Georgia, Plains sprouted in the late nineteenth century when the Seaboard Railroad came to the area. The locals are proud, hardworking people who love the pine trees, peanut fields, and magnolias that populate the area. They will also tell you about the gnats, but only because they share space with them. Some call them "flying teeth" because they bite instead of sting. They go through screen doors and make life miserable for anyone who thinks they can wear shorts when the gnats are around.

Mrs. Olsen liked it in Plains. She knew most of the people in their church, and she was especially proud that the thirty-ninth President of the United States came from there. Although small, they were on the map. It was the best of both worlds, as far as she was concerned.

But it was hot. Even though she was born just up the street in Americus, she never got used to the hot and humid summers. She didn't think anyone did. She appreciated the mild winters, and she did a lot outside during that time of year. She liked to visit Americus for fun and shopping. Sometimes she would convince the whole family to go with her, usually baiting them with the possibility of going to a movie or doing something that appealed to all of them. But summers kept her indoors most of the time. She would sew, read, and work on different projects for the church's women's group. When she did leave her air-conditioned home, it was to drive in her air-conditioned car to the air-conditioned store or to visit someone in their air-conditioned home.

Jack's plan was going to change everything. It wasn't like she could just jump in the car and visit Jack without serious planning. He could see her eyes watering. She was trying not to show her feelings, but she was so very bad at that. Her face was flush, and it looked like her eyelids were about to release a torrent of tears. Don and Becky just sat there watching, taking it all in.

"Son, Detroit is not just a few hours down the road. And it's a dangerous place."

Jack had anticipated that. He was ready.

"I know, but Dad, every place can be dangerous. It depends to a great degree upon the decisions I make and who I hang out with. You can count on me to remember the great life lessons you taught me."

Jack thought he might have gone too far with that last part. His father could smell a condescending remark a mile away. Jack tried to regroup. "And, Dad, I already have plans to come home for all the holidays and special events. I'm not going to drop off the face of the earth."

"So, who is this friend of yours?"

"That would be Willy. Actually, his full name is William James III. He was named after his father, and his father was named after his father." Mr. Olsen smiled inwardly. He could tell Jack was nervous. He always tried to be very specific when he was nervous.

"And how do you know him?"

"We met when he was a sophomore and I was a freshman. His parents sent him to live down here for a year so he could get to know his mother's side of the family. He actually stayed a year and a half, but then decided to go back and finish high school back home. We kept in touch, and he tells me that he will probably take over his Dad's business when he graduates from college. If I go up there, I can get a job with his father's business and maybe even work my way up in the company."

Jack's father thought for just a moment, then unleashed a torrent of thoughts. "You might be convinced in your own mind, but that's the thing about deception. No one here thinks that you will be able to do what you just said. Employers do not let all their workers off on all the holidays, and that job with your friend is not a sure thing. Life doesn't guarantee that you will not run into unforeseen circumstances that will cost you dearly, even your life. And as far as the syrupy comment about the 'great life lessons I taught you,' you have yet to demonstrate in this more protected environment that you are able or willing to apply them."

Jack could feel himself getting angry. *When is he ever going to cut me some slack?* was what kept running through his head. He couldn't think of any comeback that wouldn't land him in trouble. He certainly did not want to win the battle and lose the war.

His father continued. "How do you expect to finance this great adventure of yours?" Jack didn't know if he was being cynical, or if his father thought this was a temporary thing that Jack had just thought up. Jack knew he could not let his father see his growing anger.

"Dad," he said as calmly and with as grown-up a tone as he could, "I know that you and Mom have sacrificed to set aside money for our future education. Since I am not going off to college right away, I was hoping that you would be willing to give me my share now. It would be the seed money that would help me get started in life, and I promise that I will go to college later on my own dime."

The air dripped with tension. If Dad agreed to this, who was to say that Don and Becky wouldn't try to go the same route? Parents know that life can take unplanned twists and turns. What one thinks is going to happen often turns out much different. But here Jack's father faced his oldest son, at age seventeen, certain he knew everything about life that could possibly be known. How could he communicate to his son the numerous blind sides to his plans?

Jack's father thought back to when he left home. He, too, had great hopes and expectations. In his case reality hit him in the face in the person of Drill Sergeant Johnson. A slight smile crossed his face merely at the thought. He could smile now, but back then it seemed like his well-ordered world had come apart. And it had, for the purpose of Drill Sergeant Johnson was to tear down idealistic young men and make soldiers of them. He hated it then, but now, these many years later, he was so grateful he had had a man like Sergeant Johnson in his life. The lessons he learned had served him well through the years.

Jack didn't have the benefit of such hindsight. To him, the future was his oyster. All he had to do was reach out and take it.

"Son, let me think about this."

What!? That was it? "Let me think about this?" What was there to think about? Jack was baffled by his father's answer. He had presented his case—and quite well, he thought. The money eventually was going to be his anyway. What was so hard about acknowledging that Jack knew what he was doing and getting on with it? Jack was nearly incensed. One would think a man who raised a family and was responsible for millions of dollars of stuff and could hire and fire people could make a decision on something so clear and easy.

What Jack didn't know, and should have, was that his father didn't make important decisions without consulting his most important advisor: Mom. Jack had seen this pattern work itself out many times through the years. Where to live, what houses and cars to buy, where to send the kids to school, what investments to make, and many more decisions were made by his parents as a team. There was a saying Jack heard back in church as a kid during one of those times when it appeared he wasn't paying attention (but very much had been): "The man may be the head of the house, but the woman is the neck that turns the head." In some odd way, it seemed both funny and true. He had seen this truth lived out in his family across the years.

But now, in this moment, Jack knew better than to argue. Following dinner, they all left the table, and Jack wondered how much of his frustration his parents could see on his face. He was not known to hide his feelings well.

And then he realized Don and Becky were following him to his room! They wanted to do their own assessment of what had just happened and figure out what would happen next.

"Wow, Jack. Are you crazy?" he heard one of them saying. Both started shooting more questions at him.

"How are you going to get there? You don't have a car, and when you get there, how are you going to get around?"

"Mom and Dad are willing for you to live here, and pay for college. You get free food, a warm bed—all the things of home. Why would you give up such a cush gig?"

That last one was from Don. Becky chimed in: "What about Susan? Have you talked to her about this? Is she going with you? Are you going to break up?" Her questions came faster than Jack could think.

Between Don's condescending attitude and Becky's machine-gun questions, Jack's head was about to explode.

"Leave me alone! Get out of here! I don't have to answer to you! You're not the boss of me!" He picked up a shoe to throw at them as they dashed out of his room.

"Know it alls! That's what they are." Jack was not happy to have his fifteen-year-old brother and almost fourteen-year-old sister give him life advice. It was none of their business.

The truth was that Jack *hadn't* thought about all these things—and more. He thought that maybe when he got to Detroit he would use public transportation until he saved enough for a used car. But he hadn't thought about car and medical insurance, or deposits for rent and utilities, or ongoing costs for a phone, food—all the things one needs to live day to day. And he certainly hadn't thought about what he was going to do about his girlfriend, Susan. *One can't think of everything,* he dismissively told himself.

* * * * *

It was only a few days—but seemed like a lifetime—before Dad brought up the subject again. Jack dared not bring it up before. When his father said he was going to have to think about it, Jack knew he would get back to him in his own good time. Any perceived pressure, real or otherwise, from Jack would not earn him any points, and would possibly derail his plans.

A few days later, Jack got his answer. His father found him outside raking leaves and motioned for him to pause for a minute. Then, once again, he had quite the speech prepared.

"Jack, before your mother and I had children, we decided that we would raise adults. By that I mean that we would not raise our children to remain as children. We've seen parents who sheltered and hovered over their kids too much. They wouldn't let them play sports because they were afraid they would get hurt. Even when they allowed them to play sports, they insisted that all kids should get some kind of award for just showing up. They did not discipline them because they did not want to 'stifle their creativity.' They came to their defense because they refused to believe that their little boy or girl were capable of doing wrong. They wanted to be their best friends instead of their parents. There are no boundaries or responsibilities, and no consistency in the kids' lives. So these kids are never prepared to leave the nest and succeed in the adult world, where not everyone is a winner, and where your employer doesn't care that you got your feelings hurt by something someone said.

"Your mother and I determined that our children would be ready for real life. We have given you the covering of our love and security in an atmosphere that allowed you to experiment and learn. We have been willing to underwrite your mistakes within what we believed to be caring and reasonable boundaries. And we have done it, knowing all along that, one day, you would leave the nest and learn to fly on your own. And this is where the challenge lies for me. I am not convinced you are ready to be on your own."

He put his hand up as Jack was about to interrupt and assert that he was certainly ready to move on and into the adult world. Jack certainly wasn't going to tell him how he was chafing under his dad's "covering of love and security." But Jack knew that if he didn't get his father to give him his share of his parents' savings for him . . . well, it seemed to Jack that he would never get out from under their wing. It was like he would be an indentured slave—forever. However, Jack also knew—quite well—not to try to speak over his dad's raised hand.

"Life is risk management," his dad went on, and seemed quite preachy in doing so, Jack thought. "You may not entirely appreciate this now, but your mother and I know that you will never truly be ready to be on your own because you cannot predict with certainty what the future will bring. I take a risk every time I go to work, because there is no guarantee that I will return home. I take that risk because I think it is worth it to provide for my family. To put it another way, if you are holding onto something with your hand, you cannot grab anything else with that hand until you let go of what you are then holding. I think that what you want to do is let go of what you have and reach for something new. That is painful for any parent who loves their child and has seen them live through the cuts and scrapes and disappointments of youth, all the things that are part of growing up.

In the end, Jack, the truth is that parents are unsure of so many things when it comes to raising children. They do the best they know how, but they see quickly that they lack a lot of skills."

Jack's dad shifted his feet for a short pause. Jack leaned on his rake, trying to stay calm.

"I'm sorry. I don't mean to ramble or preach. You want to leave. So be it. You want a portion of the money that we set aside for your education. Although I don't want to do it, for reasons that you may not grasp now, I will give you your share."

Jack's dad went on to share what he undoubtedly thought were more pearls of wisdom of what he could expect in Detroit, the challenges he would face, and how to deal with them—but Jack wasn't listening, not really. His mind had moved on. He could see his dad's lips moving, but that was all. His mind was already swimming with the realization that he was going to—there was no other way to say it—be given a good chunk of money. *He was going to be free.*

Jack had a desire rise up in him that he hadn't experienced in years. Despite his utter lack of respect for his dad's "life lessons," he wanted to reach over and give his dad the biggest hug ever. But that would not have been cool. It would not be consistent, he reasoned, with the very independence he was trying to project. He did thank his father, and sought to conclude their time together . . . when he thought he saw his dad's eyes tearing up.

Jack got out of there and rushed back into the house, barely missing knocking his sister down in the doorway. He ran into his mother in the kitchen as she was getting ready to head out for some shopping. He gave her the biggest hug he could and kissed her all over her face, thanking her profusely, and then darted to his room to continue working on his plans.

The leaves could wait.

THREE

Making Plans

Jack's school counselor had also been his Sunday school teacher. Mr. Simpson had known Jack for a long time, first as his teacher at church when he was twelve, and now as his senior class counselor. What he was observing in Jack was the natural itch that hits boys about the time they graduate from high school. Jack wanted to be on his own, to experience life. He had grand ideas, and they tended to fog his common sense.

"Jack, are you at least going to community college?" his counselor asked him one afternoon. It was too late for Jack to submit paperwork for four-year colleges. Although his grades weren't the best, they were still good enough to get into some colleges; he just didn't have the desire. Life was waiting for him. Jack reasoned that he couldn't waste valuable time going to college.

"Mr. Simpson, we have already been over this," Jack answered. "I'm holding off on going to college. Maybe I'll go in a few years." Simpson knew Jack was only fooling himself. Statistics showed that most high school seniors who delay going to college never go. It would be a shame for Jack to miss out.

"Yes, we have discussed this, but I'm waiting for you to get back in your right mind," Mr. Simpson said with a slight chuckle, trying to keep things light. "You told me that your parents set aside money for you to go to college. You and I know that had to be a sacrifice for them. I've also told you that you have the grades and the school record that colleges are looking for. I bet we could have gotten you ten acceptances if you would have submitted the applications in time. No one knows how much scholarship money you missed out on."

"Well, I have a different idea. If my father will give me the college money to invest, I'll multiply it many times over, and I'll be able to go to college on my terms."

That was the thing with Jack. He wanted life his way. He just didn't realize life doesn't work that way.

"Jack, I hope you will reconsider," Mr. Simpson said to him in measured terms. "Your father is not against you. In fact, he is for you and against anything that might come against you. He is giving you good advice. As a school counselor, I can tell you there are lots of people who would love to be in your situation, with the blessings you have. You may not see it, but you are throwing opportunity away."

Jack thought for a moment before answering. Mr. Simpson had always looked out for him. He owed his counselor a lot. Jack knew Mr. Simpson believed he was giving him good advice, but Jack was just as sure his senior counselor was being blinded by his training and bias.

"Look, I really appreciate what you're trying to do," Jack finally answered. "I really do. You've been nothing but good to me. But I have to be me. I can't live my life if I'm always trying to live up to others' expectations. I hope you understand. Maybe I'm wrong in going this way, but when all is said and done, it's my life and my decision. I'll get through it, and who knows? I may surprise you."

Mr. Simpson could see that any further discussion would be a waste of time, and might even end up alienating Jack. He wanted to be available to help Jack pick up the pieces if he crashed and burned.

"OK. It's your life, your decision. I won't bring it up again. Keep in touch, and let me know how things turn out for you." With that, they walked to the door, shook hands, and Jack headed to his father's car, which he had borrowed for school that day.

Jack wasn't the only one facing decisions. Susan faced them as well. Her parents had high hopes for her to go to college, and she had always wanted to work in the medical field. She wanted to study pre-med and maybe get a job in the medical field to find the area she enjoyed most before committing to years of study. Even for a young woman, Jack knew, she was mature for her age.

Susan hadn't meant to fall for Jack. Boys can complicate things quickly. She met him through Becky. The two girls became friends in the seventh grade when they played on the school basketball team. They hung out together, and like most girls, shared every thought. The attraction between Jack and Susan grew slowly in the two years Susan knew Becky. Then "one day" the chemistry of young love struck them both. After that, it was seldom anyone saw them apart. Becky got a little jealous; she was seeing less of Susan by herself, but she figured this was the way life went. She hoped her brother and Susan would be happy, and that they wouldn't break each other's hearts.

Susan's father wasn't sold on Jack. He remembered his own youth, how boys thought about girls, and he didn't like it a bit that he now had to contend with a young upstart for his daughter's attention. Even though Susan loved her parents, she too was trying to assert her independence. It would be a long time before she would tell her dad about the time Jack almost killed them both when he was driving his father's car with Susan in the passenger seat. He got distracted talking to Susan, and when he realized he was heading into a sharp curve, it was nearly too late. He put the brakes on at the same time he swerved the car, and they almost ended up going over a cliff when the car skidded on loose gravel. Jack had moments like that, times when it seemed he almost had someone watching over him. Anyway, if her dad found out about that incident, Susan was certain she would not be allowed to go out with Jack again. Her father already had a bit of the "helicopter dad" in him, and this sometimes put a strain on their relationship. The bottom line was, he just didn't trust Jack. His daughter was young. For all her maturity, she didn't have the life experience that only time provides. Susan's father knew the raging hormones of young men, and he was determined not to let some young buck break his daughter's heart.

One afternoon, Susan told her mom she was going to Becky's house.

Her mom knew that if Susan told her father where she was going, she would have to run through a gauntlet of questions. "Will Jack be there?" "When are you coming home?" "Why are you going now?

Weren't you just there yesterday?" "Can't Becky come over here?" On and on it would go. It would almost be better if Susan asked to go an hour earlier just to have enough time to answer all the questions. And they were always the same. The insecurity of fathers concerning their daughters . . . Susan never heard him give the third degree to her brother this way. It seemed all she ever heard him say to her brother was something like "be careful out there."

Susan's mom wasn't naïve. She knew what was going on, and she knew her daughter. She had given her enough freedom to grow and experience life, but not enough rope to hang herself. She also knew her husband, and his desire to protect his family was one of the things that drew her to him. He wasn't always good with words, but his heart was as big as Dallas.

Susan's mom had simple instructions. "When you get there, ask Becky's mom to call me. I'd like to finalize our plans for the housing association meeting." This was her way of killing two birds with one stone. She would know Susan had arrived safe, and she would be able to catch up with Becky's mom, whom she had gotten to know quite well over the years, partly because of the relationships between their children.

Susan did want to visit with Becky, but she was really going to see her boyfriend. In fact, as soon as she was able to catch up with Becky, she would be looking for a way to spend the rest of the evening hanging out with Jack. This was convenient. There was no cost to either of them, and since they weren't doing anything crazy, they weren't risking anything with the parents. It was win-win-win. Susan got to see Becky and Jack, plus impress her family with the steady and responsible relationship she had with Jack.

Susan and Becky could read each other's minds—and body language. Something was not right during this visit. Becky was much more reserved, almost introverted, and to a degree Susan had not seen before. Susan's attempts to break through were met with a sad yet determined resistance that seemed to indicate Becky did not want to be involved in something.

"Becky, what's up? You're not talking."

"Nuthin. Nuthin's wrong." Becky was never a good liar. Susan could see something was up. Had Susan said or done something to offend her? Did someone at school spread some vicious rumor? Susan's mind began to whirl with all the possibilities. Each possible scenario would require a different response. She certainly didn't want to do or say anything to hurt Becky. They were BFFs, and nothing would ever change that. It was obvious to Susan that Becky was hurting about something, and it was her responsibility to stand with her, whatever it was. Maybe it was boy problems. That wouldn't be unusual, except that Becky had never told her that she liked anyone in particular, and that was a piece of information Becky wouldn't have kept from her best friend.

"Becky, you and I are best friends forever," Susan said. "We have gone through a lot together. You have to tell me what's bothering you. I can't help if I don't know what it is."

"It's not me, Susan." Susan could see that Becky was on the verge of tears. "It's . . ."

"What?" Susan could hear her voice getting louder and more demanding. There was a tinge of frustration, if not anger.

"Talk to Jack."

Talk to Jack? What did that mean? What had Jack done? All sorts of things went through her mind, and none of them were good. If Jack had hurt Becky, she would surely hurt him. But that didn't make sense. Sure, Jack could be impulsive, but he loved his sister. He would do anything for her. As the oldest, he seemed to always be watching over her. Sometimes he acted like a younger version of Susan's father.

"Where is he?" Susan asked. She had noticed that the car wasn't there when she arrived, but she also thought it likely Becky's father was still at work.

"He took Dad into work this morning. He got permission to use the car to run some errands. He should be back before it's time to pick Dad up."

This was sounding weirder and weirder, and Susan began to wonder if Becky was lying to her in a feeble attempt to hide something. Regardless, just as she was about to drill her friend with more questions, they heard the car pull in the driveway. She was tired of trying to pry information from her friend; she would get it herself. It didn't take a rocket scientist to see that this—whatever it was—upset Becky, and Susan now knew that Jack had something to do with it.

Jack was in trouble with Susan, and neither of them knew why. He slid out of the car with a couple of bags. She could tell he had some groceries, but wasn't sure what the other bag held.

Susan was nervous, and first thought of running out and confronting Jack. Thinking better of it, she willed herself to greet him with a smile and a hug, asked him how he was doing, and walked back in the house with him. His mother took the groceries, put them away, and continued what she was doing.

Mrs. Olsen was like a second mother to Susan. One of Susan's strengths was that she observed people. She learned a lot from watching Jack's mother. She had a way of always being there but never letting on that she heard or knew most of what was going on. When the kids were little, they were surprised when she knew things they thought she didn't. With wide eyes, they would ask, "How did you know that?"

"Why, that's simple," Mom would say. "You can't hide anything from Mom. See all this hair? Under all this hair in the back of my head are two eyes that come out when you are doing something you shouldn't be doing. All mothers have eyes in the back of their heads." The kids had never been sure about their dad, though. His hair was a lot shorter than Mom's, and they never saw any eyes on the back of his head. As they got older, they knew to respect authority because it was the right thing to do.

Susan knew enough not to get in Jack's face about what was going on. She didn't want to say something she might regret later. No, this would have to be much more subtle. Taking a deep breath and counting to—almost—ten, she decided to approach him with small talk about how he was doing, that she missed him, and so on. After a few minutes, she was convinced. Something was going on, and she was the only one not invited to the party.

Jack hadn't told Susan what he was planning for his future; Susan only knew he wasn't happy at home and wanted to go out on his own. Maybe that was because he had not really thought it through. Part of growing up is understanding that decisions you make have second- and third-order effects. In other words, decisions do not stand on their own without affecting others. It's like throwing a stone in a pond.

It makes an initial splash, but there are ripples that move out from the initial impression and affect the rest of the water. It takes a while for young people to grasp this concept, and men in particular seem to learn it later than women. Susan could only guess that this was the adventuresome spirit guys get. They seem to want to go out and conquer the world. But Susan never imagined what Jack had in mind.

Jack had been out that morning researching his move. Sure, he had thought about doing it for the longest time, but his focus up to now had been on getting his share of his parents' set-aside college money. Now that he had that, he needed to start putting some thought into the actual details of the move. The devil is in the details, they say. What was the best way to do this? Should he fly and rent a car on the other end? How much would it cost to fly? Should he just rent or lease a car? Should he buy a car? New or used? How much would it cost to move into an apartment by himself, or should he share one with his friend? He assumed he had a job waiting—his friend Will had promised one—but he was beginning to wonder if he needed to double-check that, too.

Suddenly, the issues were getting very real to Jack.

After he received some basic information from his father, Jack found out that all the money he was going to receive was not going to pay for all the things he was now realizing he would need! When he crunched the numbers, he came up with unexpected conclusions. He would have to buy the cheapest and most reliable car he could get before he left. Flying to Detroit and then renting a car would be too expensive. Buying a car in Detroit would be too uncertain. He wasn't familiar with car dealers in the area, and at least here in Plains, Georgia he could count on decent advice from people he knew.

His friends at school got new cars for graduation, but that was not going to happen for Jack. Had he stopped to think about this, however—and he hadn't—he would realize that his friends and their families were always in debt. They lived from paycheck to paycheck. His parents didn't have the newest and most expensive things, but they bought quality. They were frugal, but they weren't cheap. They didn't owe anyone, and they had enough money to be able to give to worthy causes. It brought joy to them to be able to help others in need. As generous as they were, they still had enough money set aside for the proverbial rainy day.

Moving into an apartment was going to be expensive—much more than Jack expected. After some research of apartments in the area of Detroit he was looking at—a decently safe neighborhood a good bit away from the downtown, he thought—Jack learned that he had to come up with the first and last month's rent. If that was all, that alone would have been a shock to his system. He also learned he would have to furnish the apartment, and that meant buying furniture and having it delivered (unless he could borrow a truck from someone he could quickly meet, or get lucky enough to know). Even if he bought used items online, he would still have to find a way to get the items home. But that wasn't all. He had to have all the utilities turned on or taken care of. And all of these required deposits. Forget about cable or satellite TV. He reasoned that he had to have Internet for many things—including job searches if the job did not pan out—but it was either that or his phone expenses, so he decided he needed a phone more. At least this one was a wise choice: he would learn later the phone was a requirement for potential employers.

Jack still hadn't thought so many things through. He would have to pay for insurance, and there was the "minor" challenge of feeding himself, plus the costs of regular maintenance or payments on anything he owned or was buying via installments. Of course, that meant getting credit, which he didn't have, and couldn't get because he wasn't buying anything on credit, which he didn't have, and couldn't get because... All in all, it was becoming quite serious; life was getting real. It didn't look like anything he had seen on TV or imagined from his video games.

As he looked at the money he would have, and the costs of starting out on his own, he wondered how people ever left home. People were staying with their parents more and more after graduating from school, and he was beginning to understand why. Even if Willy and he shared expenses, it was still going to be much harder than he hoped.

There was also the problem of Susan. Interesting that he never thought of her as a problem before. He had grown to love her, as much as a 17-year-old knows about love. Their relationship had grown as they had grown. They were full of youthful energy and the dreams that accompany it. They never spoke of a future together, but it was always in the background. Their parents were friends, and although Susan's father didn't trust Jack, it wasn't because he thought Jack was a bad kid. It was just because he still was a kid and somewhat immature for his age. Lack of maturity can result in bad decisions, and Larry Johnson didn't want his daughter to suffer for it. He would rather wait for young Jack to become a responsible young man before he trusted his little girl to him. He was still getting over the time Jack brought his daughter (and like a lot of dads, he still thought of her as Daddy's little girl) home fifteen minutes late after a date. Fifteen minutes might not have seen much to Jack, but it was a lifetime for Larry Johnson. Just another reason not to trust this boy—a well-meaning kid, all in all, but still a *boy*. If he couldn't be responsible enough to tell time, he wasn't ready for Mr. Johnson's princess.

Jack and Susan had always approached problems together. Granted, what they perceived to be problems were mere blips on the screen of life, but in their world, they were serious enough that they felt they had be united in dealing with them. This was different, though. Jack was in the middle of making a major change in his life, and he had never discussed it with Susan. He did not know how he was going to bring the subject up, and how she was going to take it. The details of the upcoming move, plus the unknown repercussions on his relationship with Susan and her family, were suddenly overwhelming.

* * * * *

After getting the first heavy vibe from Becky, Susan held out as long as she could. To her credit, she gave Jack most of the rest of that afternoon to fill her in on the big secret. But his mind was somewhere else. Susan could tell something was in the air, and it was getting close to the time Jack had to pick up his father from work. It was either now or she was going to have to wait till tomorrow to try to find out what was going on. And that was not going to happen. In the few minutes she had left with him before Jack had to take off, while sitting on Jack's back porch, she dived in.

"Jack, when I came here today, Becky was not her usual self. She was reserved and didn't seem to want to talk like we usually do. I tried all afternoon to get her to tell me what was bothering her, and all I got from her was 'talk to Jack.' What's going on, Jack? What is it that she doesn't want to tell me?" She thought about pointing out that Jack also was acting strange, but thought better of it. She would only play that card if Jack pushed her to it.

"I don't know what's bothering her. She's Becky. She gets like this all the time. I'm surprised you haven't noticed this about her before now." Jack was as bad at lying as his sister. Susan could tell Jack was squirming. He wasn't ready to talk about what was going on, but that was not going to stop her. If there was one thing she was better at than him, it was persistence. So, she continued questioning him, always stopping just short of what would be considered nagging, but nonetheless continuing until she got what she wanted. Jack knew this, and he knew it was only a matter of time before he would give in. He now wished he hadn't kept this from her. He did want a future with Susan, but he was afraid she would try to talk him out of moving to Detroit. Looking back on it, he wondered how he concluded that he would tell her later without any problems. The truth was he hadn't *considered* telling her. This action, from Jack, was a bit like closing your eyes and hoping no one sees you.

Susan backed off for a few minutes—but only a few. Jack would change the subject or give some response that revealed little, but all this showed was that his defenses were weakening. Jack's mother was in the kitchen, and every once in a while, from their vantage point on the porch, Susan thought she could see a small smile cross Mrs. Olsen's face. Susan didn't know if she was smiling about something else or if the "eyes in the back of the head" were at work. (Susan often wondered if Jack's mother handled her husband in the same way. One thing was certain from years of observation by Susan: Jack's father deeply loved his wife. Sometimes, he would come up behind her and hug her and kiss her neck in his playful way. No one else wanted to see it, but he didn't care. It was obvious he felt he had won first prize in some grand contest.)

Finally, Susan decided to go big. "Jack, we can't keep talking around this. Something is going on, and you don't want to tell me. Did you do something to Becky? Because if you did, I will hurt you like you've never been hurt. Is there another girl? Do you want to break up with me?"

Jack couldn't take the pressure, and his somewhat angry response was the first crack in the dam. "No! I haven't done anything to Becky," he shot back. "Where do you come up with such crazy thoughts? I don't want to break up with you, either."

"Then why won't you tell me what's going on? Don't you trust me? Have I ever not supported you? You act like you committed some unpardonable sin or something."

Before Jack could answer, the back door opened and Jack's younger brother headed through the backyard. "Hi, Susan. Long time no see. What's it been, two days?" Donny always tried to be funny. He knew that Jack and Susan spent a lot of time together, even when she came over to see Becky. She smiled at Donny, even though she was still trying to get Jack to open up. Donny could tell the smile was forced.

"So, Jack. Did you tell her about Detroit?"

For Donny, it was one of those moments everyone has at some point. As the words were tumbling from his mouth, you could see his mind trying to keep them from spilling out. The tongue sometimes disengages from the mind. This was one of those moments for Donny.

Immediately, everyone could sense the change in atmosphere. If it had been a weather system, Jack would have felt the partly cloudy day turning to an extremely dark day with the strong possibility of thunderstorms. The faces told their own stories. Jack looked stunned, trapped. This was not what he wanted. He wanted to find the right time to break the news to Susan. Maybe they would be able to work out something where she could join him at some point. That didn't seem realistic, though, because he knew she had no desire to leave town; she was already looking forward to attending the local college. Also, he hadn't proven himself trustworthy in the eyes of her father, so chances were slim to none that their relationship had a long-term future. So Jack did the one smart thing he could in the moment: he kept his mouth shut.

Susan's face looked stunned, but intensely questioning. *Detroit?*

What did that mean? Was Jack going to Detroit? For how long? Why? What about them? Was he breaking up with her? What had she done? Now Susan was completely confused. How could all this happen? They were so close. They had been through so much. She momentarily looked back and up at the kitchen. Jack's mother was not smiling.

Jack hadn't packed the first item, and life as he knew it had suddenly changed. All these decisions. Nothing was going as he expected. He had to regroup. That didn't mean that he had to change his mind about leaving. Oh no, that was certain. He was out of there as soon as possible. *But what to do about Susan?* He didn't want to break up with her. Already he could sense that breaking up would affect both families in ways he hadn't anticipated. He could ask her to come with him, but that was almost certainly a non-starter with her heart set on going to college locally. The only thing he could think of was trying a long-distance relationship. They could text and call each other every day—that is, if he could afford to keep his cell phone. Then, maybe, she could visit him on weekends, and he could see her when he came down for holidays. This could work.

But who was Jack kidding? He was talking about someone who had the means to do these things, and one thing was for sure. He could see that he would barely have enough to provide for his basic needs, much less what would be needed to keep up a long-distance relationship.

Jack was beginning to feel trapped. Actually, he had a way out—to stay in town and start college, as Susan planned to do—but his pride would keep him from doing that. He would not cancel or delay his plans.

FOUR

Susan

While planning your life, things have a way of happening in spite of those plans. Susan got her acceptance letter to college, but it wasn't her first choice. It was also far enough away that she would have to live in a dorm, and she wouldn't be able to come home until the weekends, and then only if her student job didn't require her to work those days. Susan was also beginning to sense that her and Jack's relationship was coming to an end. She didn't want their relationship to end, but it was beyond her control. Jack hadn't talked with her before he made his big plans, and maybe being accepted by this college was God's way of telling her to move on with her life.

When Susan had important things to consider, she usually talked to her mother. Once in a while, her father would join the conversation. They never pushed her to make a particular decision, but instead tried to give her enough information and their wisdom so she could make wise choices. This was one of those times. Afterward, when she was by herself contemplating all that she had experienced and heard, she did one more thing. She prayed. It wasn't something she did often, although no one in her family discouraged her from praying. Her experience with praying had mostly been limited to family meal times when she was asked to return the thanks.

School, on the other hand, was totally different. When prayer was mentioned at all, it was usually in a negative way. It was usually linked with some wisecrack about "holy rollers" or "right wing fundamentalists" or "haters." She didn't know where she stood on many issues of the day, but it seemed to her that people who were sincere about their belief in God were generally good people. She had never been around anyone who fit the descriptions that some of her friends described. She got the feeling that they were parroting what they had heard, not what they had seen for themselves. Most of the teachers were the same. Not to say that there weren't others like her, who believed in a higher power. There were, but for the most part, they remained silent. And this only served to make her wonder how strong their convictions were if they stayed quiet while others criticized their faith. Maybe they didn't have convictions as strong as those of nonbelievers. But who was she to criticize? She didn't speak up either. She knew that if she would somehow be arrested for being a believer, people would be surprised. She never spoke or did anything that would give anyone the slightest hint that she was different in her beliefs than the average person.

    The situation with Jack and college did accomplish one positive thing. It pushed Susan to look at herself again. Her entire person, not just her physical looks. Although she did start there. As a child, she believed she could learn to make her eyes twinkle and her teeth sparkle just like she saw on TV. Eventually, she realized that those twinkles and sparkles were only there because of special effects. She smiled when she thought about how naive she was back then. She had grown up considerably, and this time was a serious moment in her life.

    Back in her room, Susan stared at herself in the full-length mirror she always looked at before going out. Before, she wanted to make sure that every hair was in place, that the outfit was the right one for the occasion, that she didn't have her dress caught in her pantyhose or something like that. But now she was looking at herself differently. She was trying to see what was inside, beyond the makeup, beyond the smile, beyond the charm.

    She had learned to use makeup for several reasons. Although it took time, she wanted her face to look as nice and healthy as possible. She had developed the occasional pimple, usually at the wrong time. Makeup helped cover it up. She also noticed that she was growing up to be an average-looking person—not as bad as some, but not the beauty queen she had hoped. Why are girls so caught up in their self-image? Darn boys! Although, she had read somewhere that men spend more time than women looking at themselves in the mirror. Both genders could do with a little less vanity, she figured. Anyway, there was not much to work with in her case, Susan figured, so she wanted to make the best use of what she had. Competition among girls was fierce. She had learned to be charming when she didn't feel charming. She had learned to paste on a smile when the occasion required it. Yes, indeed, she was cute . . . and charming—and empty inside.

Jack was a little wilder than other boys she had dated. Somewhere along the way, she had decided she wasn't interested in "safe" boys. Jack was a greater challenge. He was unpredictable, like a wild stallion. One minute he would be going full speed, and then suddenly he would switch directions. You never knew what he might do next. It was both thrilling and dangerous at the same time. Maybe this was Susan's way of making up for what she perceived to be her own boring life. She went to school. She worked part-time. She did what was expected of her. She had never done anything wild and crazy, unless you count the time she went out with the church youth group and toilet papered the tree in front of the youth pastor's house. In short, Susan was the stereotypical good girl. Or maybe she wanted to help Jack find his way. She was always the one who would take in the baby bird that fell out of the nest in the spring, or the stray dog that showed up in the neighborhood. She was the girl you would see putting up posters all over town with a picture of the latest lost animal she had found, that she was now looking for its rightful owner.

In a way, Jack was like a lost puppy. He wanted to have fun and yet wanted everyone to take him serious. He had great short-term plans that never panned out because he lived in the now, and he never considered the long-term results of his great ideas. Perhaps Susan saw it as her role to bring balance to his life, and in a reciprocal way, some excitement into hers.

This was no way to live. As she looked in the mirror, Susan realized she was living for all the wrong reasons. Her value was not dependent on how she looked. She was good all by herself. This became a revelation to her. All of her life, when people saw her for the first time, or even later, people would always say something about how pretty she was, even if she just came in from playing in the dirt. "Oh, isn't she cute?" they would say. "How's our pretty girl today?" "You are such a pretty girl." "You are going to break many boys' hearts someday." It was all about how she looked. No wonder she got the message that she was only as good as her looks. She never heard those kinds of things said to her brother. He would hear things like "How's my little man today?" "Show me your muscle. Ooh, yeah, that's big." "While I'm gone, you're the man of the house. Be sure to take care of your mom and little sister." She understood that boys and girls are different. She was no feminist, but she was not a dumb blonde either, not even a bleached one. She made better grades than her brother, for starters. She didn't want to compare herself with him; that would be wrong. She had to look at herself and figure out who she was.

She mentally tore down the façade she had built around herself. Her looks did not determine her value. Maybe she had given into peer pressure and was now using too much makeup and crossing the line of immodesty with some of her clothing choices. Charm is fine, but it is too easy to use to manipulate people and situations. Too much of it is like putting too much sugar in a recipe. It gets sickeningly sweet and actually repels people instead of attracting them. Smiles were similar. The plastic smile had to go. A forced smile shows dishonesty more than it shows good manners. She had to find a way to be gracious without being deceptive. And then there was the worst personal stumbling block, in her mind: her tongue. Susan thought long and hard about the many times she said things about people and to people that hurt them. Gossip was only the tip of the iceberg. She seemed to have an uncontrollable need to build herself up and tear others down. Of course, she would not admit that before now. She would have just said that she was being analytical, or truthful, that her motives were pure, that she was just trying to make things or people better, and that she didn't mean to hurt others. But now the scales were coming off her eyes.

It's amazing, Susan thought, *how the heart can deceive.* She didn't really *want* to make people or things better. She didn't really care about the lost animals she helped bring back to health or made other efforts for, like trying to find their rightful owners. She didn't really care about Jack, if she was honest. At least not in the way she thought she did. Jack was a tool. She was hoping he would fill what was missing in her life. What she was now beginning to realize was that he could not fill the void in her life—no one could. Not Jack, not her brother, not Becky, not her parents. No one. As she thought about things even more, she realized her good grades, as important as they were, were not the answer. There were a lot of smart people who were equally unfulfilled and unhappy, who led lives of empty desperation. Her job was not the answer. She knew enough to know that, although money might make some things possible and easier, too many people get caught up in chasing after it until, one day, they realize *they* have been caught by *it*—and become its slave.

All of this felt like peeling an onion and pulling a scab at the same time. Susan thought her life was reasonably together—until she found herself peeling back the layers of her existence. It was painful to see herself for who she really was. She hadn't committed any terrible crimes or anything like that; in fact, she could argue that she was as good as anybody else. Even better than some. But somehow, that didn't seem right. She felt dirty. She felt wrong. Dare she say it? She felt *sinful*.

As she continued her self-evaluation, there would be times she would remember when someone hurt her. Sometimes it would be a physical injury, like the time she was playing second base on the softball team and a girl running the bases ran over her. Other times, it was the proverbial "knife in the back" incidents where she felt betrayed, often by someone she trusted. Of the two, the heart betrayals hurt the worst. By far. This, she realized, caused her to build an emotional wall around her heart. On the outside, she portrayed a caring person, sensitive to the needs of those around her. But on the inside, Susan had lost her ability to feel. She had been hurt so many times that she didn't trust anymore, and worst of all she didn't trust herself. At least when she suffered a cut or a bruise, she could see the injury. With some physical injuries, she had scars that would remind her she had been hurt there before, and yet healing had occurred. With the wounds of the heart, she had invisible scars she could not see. It eventually caused her to always keep her guard up, to not trust anyone to get close because they might see just how broken she really was.

As Susan pondered the reality of her true condition, she drifted in her thoughts to the subject of prayer. As a child, she said her prayers every night. Sometimes her father would lead her, and sometimes it was her mother. Both had their unique way of ending the storytelling and the prayers. When Mom finished, she would give Susan a hug and kiss, wish her a good night, and tell her she loved her. Dad would do the same thing, almost. He would also tuck the sheets in tightly around her, then "accidentally" tickle her in the process. She always felt loved and safe. At first, she learned to relate to God in the same way. Somehow she knew He loved her even more than her parents, and she would talk with Him as she would with her parents. It seemed He was closer to her than her own brother. But somewhere along the way, she drifted away. Maybe it was the busyness of her life, or the constant bombardment of new ideas, but at some point she began to draw away. She began to question the reality of God.

Maybe she had believed in Him in the same way someone believes in the tooth fairy. The church they attended always made sure Santa Claus showed up at Christmastime and the Easter Bunny be present for Easter and the annual Easter egg hunt. She learned, sooner than most, that these characters weren't real. So . . . maybe God wasn't real either. Maybe he was something somebody made up to scare us into being good, she reasoned. And everything she was learning at school (where her parents expected her to pay attention and get good grades) seemed to tell her that these suspicions were correct. There was no God, and science proved it.

But that was then, and this was now, and her life was much more messed up than when she believed. As she thought about it, she remembered the kids she knew in high school who had "gotten saved." That was a popular saying. They said they were "born again." Some said they had "made a commitment to Christ" or "made a decision for Christ" or some such phrase meant to indicate they were now different. They talked about repentance and sin and salvation as if these things were real. Susan didn't know enough to argue, but she could see by their lives that something had happened. They had changed. It was like they were new people. Some came to her and apologized for long-ago offenses. Some even cried, as if they had an inkling of the pain they inflicted long ago. At times, it was awkward. Some of the things they mentioned, she didn't even remember. At first she thought they were doing it because of some religious obligation they had to complete in order to please God. But she found it went deeper than that. There was a genuine love for her, a love that she sensed didn't originate with them.

As Susan looked in the mirror and contemplated all the things that were going on in her life, she decided to pray. Not like the prayers she repeated as a child, but as if there was someone in the room who could hear her. If the God of her childhood was real, she reasoned, she would see some changes. If not, she would have only wasted a few minutes, and she would not be the worse for it. She said the things some of her friends had told her. She confessed her shortcomings, asked God to forgive her, and asked Jesus to come live inside her. It was all very cerebral. She prayed, and nothing happened.

Not really wanting to spend any more time on it, she walked away from the mirror and focused her attention on other things. She had her household chores to do and a schedule to keep. She would deal with Jack later.

FIVE

Detroit at Last

Things moved quickly for the both of them. In reality, they were no longer a couple. Jack didn't officially break up with Susan, but they quit going out together other than when they were with a group. Susan continued her preparations for college, and Jack continued with his plans for Detroit.

No matter how Jack figured it, he would not be able to afford a car. He would have to use public transportation once he reached the big city. He resolved to tough it out for as long as it took. He would get a job, save money, live cheaply, and eventually get a car. He also could not afford to fly. He bought a one-way bus ticket. Late one night at the bus station, he said goodbye to his parents, Don, and Becky. Susan did not come; their relationship had pretty much died. It was late in the evening, so no one else came to see him off. This was just as well. He had burned some bridges.

When he arrived in Detroit, it was late in the evening, the bus trip had taken the better part of twenty-four hours, and he was worn out from last-minute packing and the long bus ride. For a young guy, his bones ached more than he expected.

The only friend he had in Detroit—part of the argument for his going there in the first place—met him at the bus station. William James III was his name. But Jack's trip—and life—almost ended a few minutes later. Typical young guy stuff. Talking and not paying attention to where they were going. Even with a policeman there guiding traffic, they stepped out into the street at the wrong time and almost got crushed by one of the city buses. If Jack had been a cat, he would have been at risk of quickly using up one of those nine lives.

William James III was named after his grandfather, who started the family business. His father inherited it, and now Will was expected to take it over when he graduated from college. There was only one catch. He had to graduate from college, and right now it didn't look like he would make it. It wasn't that he didn't care. He cared a lot. Sure, he did his share of staying out too late and partying a bit much, but that didn't last long. He eventually settled down and focused on his studies and preparing for his future, which would have been great except he apparently did not inherit the business gene from his father. Instead, he inherited the art gene from his mother. She had developed a following and was pretty much established as an artist. He liked that she was recognized when she went out in public—but the art did not pay the bills. Dad's construction business paid the bills. At the rate Will was going, he would qualify to work as a laborer when he graduated from college, but no smart businessman would let him anywhere near the front office with his lack of business acumen. So it now looked like his younger sister was going to inherit leadership of the company.

This wasn't all. In his efforts to focus more on his grades, Will had to cut back on his work hours, so he was unable to afford an apartment. He was glad that Jack had come to Detroit, but Will had been forced to move back in with his parents. He simply could not make ends meet, not even sharing expenses with Jack.

This was a piece of information Jack would have liked to have known before he picked up and moved all that distance. Too common among young guys, the two simply had not communicated—at least well. Or, Will had been too ashamed to admit this to Jack before his coming.

"Are you kidding me? Are you telling me I have to make it on my own or get another roommate? I don't know anybody here."

"OK, OK. I know it doesn't look good right now, but here's what we can do," Will offered. "I've talked to my folks about this. You move in with us. There is a guest room you can use, and after you get a job,

The Way Up

you can find a place. By then, maybe you'll have found a roommate."

This was not the right time for Jack to hear this. He just finished a cross-country bus ride, and he was hungry and beat. What was Will talking about, "after you get a job"?

"Willy, I thought I had a job waiting when I got here. That's what you told me six months ago when I was making plans to come up here."

Will cleared his throat. "Well, that's true. That's what I said six months ago, but business has not been good. You know that Detroit has been hit hard with the economic stuff, and my dad had to lay off some people. I asked him about it the other day, and he told me that, to be fair, he would have to rehire the people he laid off before he took on new workers."

"Even gofers?" Jack would have been happy to just get a foot in the door doing anything. He thought maybe he would work basic labor kinds of things, carrying things here and there, maybe going to pick up materials from a local lumber store. Nothing that took a lot of skills because, frankly, he didn't know anything about construction except that those who built things used hammers and nails. He didn't know that even the most menial kind of work could be extremely competitive.

"I'm sorry, Jackie. That's just the way it is," he heard Will saying. "If you had waited another six months, maybe things would have been better."

Jack had not been willing to wait. He had made up his mind, and once he made up his mind, he was not going to let anything stand in his way. That great character quality, perseverance, had mutated into stubbornness. "So, let me get this straight," Jack found himself saying as they sat in Will's car, navigating the parking lot on their way out of the bus station. "I just traveled halfway across the country to find out I have no job and no roommate. I have no way of making money to live on, and I only have a temporary place to stay. Is that the picture?"

"Well, yeah, but it's not that bad," Will said. "You have a roof over your head, you're not out on the street, and you're not going to starve." Will was right about one thing. It was not that bad. In a way, it was *worse*.

Willy's home was totally different from what Jack was used to. Willy's mother was a great artist. But she had missed the cooking gene, the cleaning gene, the organizing gene, and whatever other genes a homemaker should have. And what she did have, in addition to being a good artist, was an overabundance of sensitivity. She would cry when she saw a leaf fall off a tree. She could not distinguish between a joke and a serious comment, so she was often offended and hurt when something humorous was said, and she laughed at the most inopportune times.

And so, life in Will's house began. Jack and Will only hung out a bit. Jack found himself alone much of the time. He had no friends, no transportation when he needed it, and his money was running out. With no job skills or experience, his prospects were limited to jobs at fast food restaurants, and he was not about to stoop that low. His pride would continue to hold him back.

It was not long before he overstayed his welcome. Visitors and fish are the same in one way, the saying goes. After three days, both begin to smell. He found himself walking on eggshells around Will's mother. Will spent a lot of time at school and the library. Will's father was gone most of the time at work. Jack wondered if he used that as an excuse not to have to deal with his wife's idiosyncrasies. Add to that the unexpected waves of homesickness that enveloped Jack at times, and no, things were not that bad—they were worse.

Just as his parents had wisely anticipated, Jack was not able to come home for Christmas. They struggled with the idea of buying him tickets to come home. They eventually decided not to rescue him in that way, but did send him a little money to help him enjoy Christmas as best he could away from family. This was just what he needed. He had taken on some seasonal work at a warehouse and managed to save up a little money. It also got him out of Will's house so he didn't have to deal with the dysfunction there. The money his parents sent him was enough to complete what he needed to move into a room at a boarding house. This would at least get him out on his own and away from the craziness at Will's place. So, on New Year's Day, Jack moved in to his new place.

It was better, but still not his own apartment. He had to share much more space and time than he wanted with other people in the house. He couldn't be himself, and he had to put locks on everything he didn't want stolen. But he was closer to work, his expenses were actually less, and he was able to continue to save for an apartment.

* * * * *

Winters in Detroit can be brutal. When the weatherman says to expect eight inches of snow, you can pretty well take it to the bank that there will be two-thirds of a foot of snow. Locals are so accustomed to harsh winters that they have snowplows out right away, working constantly, when it snows. The natives say there are really only two seasons in Detroit: winter and construction. Winter because it is cold most of the year, with shorter-than-they-should-be springs, summers, and falls. Construction because, as soon as the weather allows, the road crews are out closing freeway lanes and repairing all the damage the weather and snowplows created during the winter. If Jack had known all of this and what he was going to experience here, he might have chosen a place with a warmer climate to start out his life after high school.

It was during this time—just after he moved into his new place—that he met Jason. They met at work. They were among the folks the warehouse company hired for the Christmas season. The season actually went from the first week in November into February because of all the merchandise people returned. It was interesting to Jack that people would buy gifts for people they hardly knew or even liked. Very little thought was put into gift-giving, it seemed. And he knew a lot of people worked extra during the holidays so they could at least defray some of the debt they had built up during Christmas spending money on gifts for family and friends and coworkers and acquaintances. Many of these gifts made no sense.

Jack and Jason were a lot alike. They liked to laugh, and they seemed to gather a crowd around them when they were on break at work. They started to hang out together, and they found out they had more in common with each other than with anyone else. They both wanted to get ahead, they both did not like people in authority, and they both had great plans for the future. It was not *if* they made it big—only *when*, as far as they were concerned. They were not that far apart in age. Jason was two years older. But he seemed to have much more life experience than his age would suggest. The only thing the two did not have in common was that Jason had spent time in prison and Jack had not. Jason's emotional highs and lows were a little more pronounced than Jack's. Both of them liked to have fun, but when Jason was enjoying himself, it sometimes seemed his happiness was off the charts. He would get loud and boisterous and enjoy the moment much longer than anybody else. When he was down, his countenance appeared to take on a darkness, a gloominess something like the storm clouds that suddenly appear in the rainy season.

He was physically bigger than Jack, and his well-muscled body gave away that he spent considerable time in the gym. Maybe that was what he had to do in prison to keep himself occupied. He also had a few tattoos, but Jack attributed that to prison life too. Jason never really said why he went to prison, but he was insistent that he had been set up. Jack didn't push it. After all, Jack figured, to each his own. Life wasn't fair, and Jack was certainly beginning to understand that.

For the first time since Jack left home, he was starting to enjoy his life. Jason and he hung out almost all the time. Jason had a car, so they went to a lot of places together. Jack developed a liking for classic cars, and Detroit had classic car parades almost every weekend somewhere in the area. Jason liked to go clubbing, so both of them would often end up at a club somewhere after running around the city throughout the day. But all this did not settle well with Jason's girlfriend.

When Jason got out of lockup, he went to live with a woman he had met through the "write a prisoner" program. When people go to prison, they are often abandoned by their family and friends. Jason's case fit that pattern. He did not come from a stable family; his own father spent more time in jail than out, much of it for petty crimes. As a result, he rarely could get a job, and when he did, he always managed to do something to lose it. His mother was left to raise four kids by herself. Jason was the second son, and he looked up to his older brother, who followed in his father's steps. His mother tried her hardest, but without a man in the home, the deck was stacked against her. Her first son was shot in a robbery. After that, it was only a matter of time before Jason went wrong, too. When he ended up in prison, she took his younger brother and sister and moved out west, hoping to make a new life. Jason had not heard from them since.

The "write a prisoner" program was a way for inmates to keep in touch with the outside world. Most of those who signed up were well-meaning people who believe that everyone deserves a second chance. They helped many prisoners keep their sanity during difficult times. However, in some cases, certain people should never have been allowed to participate in the program.

Margaret was not a bad person. She was just one of those people who sought through others what she lacked in herself. She also had a felt need to help others. Some would call her an enabler; others would say she was more of a rescuer. Her own life had been rough at times. Her family life had been abusive, physically and mentally. There were times she thought about running away, but she never did because she didn't want to leave her mother in bad circumstances. Maybe that was where she developed this need to help people who didn't care enough to help themselves. She had been married twice. Both times she married men who turned out to be much like her father. When he was sober, her dad seemed nearly perfect. When he was drunk, he was a mean drunk. He would lash out at her mother, or at Margaret if she was within range. He blamed all his shortcomings on them. Funny how life repeats itself. He died in an automobile accident, and her mother remarried a man just like him. And now here Margaret was— she had repeated the same thing herself.

A friend told her she could do some good by volunteering to write letters to prisoners. She thought this might be a good idea. It would give her a chance to contribute to society and help someone at the same time. She didn't have much money, and this would help give her a sense of purpose. It was her way of paying rent for the air she breathed.

They gave her three names. Jason was the only one who continued to write, and over time, a relationship developed. She did not want or expect a close relationship. She thought this relationship began for real when she went to visit Jason in prison. They didn't have much time together, and she had to speak to him through a glass and on a phone, but even then his charisma filtered through. With every succeeding visit, she began to feel like she could talk to him about anything. Before long, Margaret looked forward to spending time with him. As he got closer to being released, they were allowed to sit in a room together with a guard in the corner watching them.

She picked Jason up the day he was released and took him back to her house. It was a lower middle-class house situated in an established neighborhood. Most of the homes belonged to young families or empty nesters. There were few single people in the area. People led busy lives and tended to hide away when they were home. His moving in with her was hardly noticeable.

Their seemingly newly idyllic life did not remain idyllic long.

The imagination has a way of emphasizing the positive and playing down the negative. Both Margaret and Jason had unreal expectations. Margaret looked forward to once again having a man around the house. She yearned for conversation with someone other than herself. She expected that they would share good experiences and make memories, laughing together and discovering new things about each other. She thought they might even marry someday and grow old together. Not that she was anxious to get married; she already had two failed marriages and was beginning to think she would never find a decent man. Jason had similar, yet different, expectations. He was glad to have her to talk with, but it seemed all he wanted to talk about was making it big. He had a need to feel superior to others and felt he was falling behind. To him, Margaret was someone who could help him get to the next level. To Margaret, it became obvious after a while that he was not interested in contributing to a serious long-term relationship. Although he was charming and charismatic, he was not interested in people except for what they could do for him.

It was not long before the differences between them, which they originally found so cute and attractive, began to be the things that pulled them apart. Jason spent more and more time away from home, sometimes staying away for days. He would come home to change clothes and leave again without giving Margaret any idea where he was going or what he was doing. In a way, this was a good thing. He was going deeper into his old lifestyle, and if he ever got caught,

Margaret at least would be able to honestly answer questioning that she did not know.

But at this point, she didn't see those things. At first, she tried to help Jason see that each of them had to work on the relationship. He would agree, but they would turn out to be empty words. After a while, she noticed that he was either not willing or simply unable to put in the effort to make their relationship work. She was always the one giving in. She was the one staying up late worrying and wondering about his whereabouts and safety. She was the one receiving phone calls from people she didn't know at all hours of the day and night. She knew that he was busy, but she could never find out what he was doing. When she confronted him, he would give incomplete answers. Their conversations often degraded into arguments, and this became the dominant pattern after a while. They never became physically violent, although an outside observer wouldn't believe it. The neighbors called the police on them more than once when their yelling at each other crossed some imaginary line.

Margaret thought that maybe she was destined to pick losers. Or maybe it was all her fault. What was wrong with her that she always seemed to end up with men who disregarded her needs? As a child, she used to imagine that she was a princess, that her prince was just around the corner. What had happened to her prince? Was she that bad of a person? Certainly, there must be something wrong with her. The world is made up of winners and losers, her father used to say when he was around. To Margaret, it was beginning to look like she was the latter.

*****

But Margaret had this going for her: she had a friend who didn't let her dwell on this kind of negativity. Her friend Miriam had a similar background to hers, and Miriam also had been going the wrong way in life for awhile. She got involved with the wrong kinds of people, made dumb decisions, and no matter how hard she tried, nothing seemed to work out for her. That is, until one day at the laundromat. She found herself reading a little religious booklet that someone—

no doubt purposely—had left behind. Her initial reaction was one of scorn. "Stupid Christians. Some people will do anything to avoid dealing with reality," she muttered. Unexpectedly, she realized the last part of her thought might apply to her as well. *What did that mean?* Miriam wondered. Could there be a reality she was not aware of? She put the laundry from the washer into the dryers and continued thinking about it.

It did not happen overnight, but not too long afterward, that Miriam had a religious conversion. She prayed "the prayer" one day when she was alone in her apartment. She felt a big weight lift, and her mind seemed to clear. Suddenly, she felt a wave of emotion rise up from deep inside, and she started to cry. No, Miriam started to wail. All of the feelings she had suppressed for so long came to the surface. Her boyfriend was at work, so she was alone in their apartment. She didn't know how long she stayed on the floor, but she remembered that she felt like she couldn't stop crying. She confessed every sin she could remember committing and even confessed to some she wasn't sure she had committed. She forgave everyone who had hurt her. She worshipped. All of this seemed strange to her because she had never been in a church or read a Bible. She lost track of time, and by the time she stopped, it was dark outside. She was tired, but she felt clean, like God had cleaned her from the inside. And she was happy. She didn't remember the last time she was truly happy.

Not really sure what to do next, Miriam thought that maybe she should find a church to attend. She didn't know it at the time, but the church she visited was one of those churches that believed the Bible is true and that God is active in the world today. She didn't know much, but she knew God had become real to her, and she was going to do all in her power to know Him better.

It was quite exciting to her, although not without its challenges and disappointments. The more she learned of her new faith, the more she wanted to share with others. It was like she had discovered the cure to some dreaded disease, and she would be wrong not to share it. Surprisingly to her, not everyone wanted to hear the cure. Some people looked at her strange, others openly chastised her, and some warned her about getting too religious. They would tell her that a little religion goes a long way, but too much could make you crazy. The most interesting thing she noticed was that a lot of her friends quit being around her. The reactions to her newfound faith were varied; some thought it was good for her, but not something they were interested in. Some thought she had gone weird. Some asked her more questions, and some actually began to explore Christ. Perhaps one of the best things she noticed was that although she lost a considerable number of friends, she felt like she had finally found a family.

Margaret was one of those who had not thrown her to the curb. They didn't hang out as much, but Margaret felt drawn to her in some inexplicable way. Miriam was the one person Margaret could talk to when she needed good advice. The fact that she had become a Christian seemed to somehow make her a better counselor. One particular day, Margaret needed to speak to Miriam.

"Jason and I had another fight tonight. He just left, and I'm sure he won't be back before morning," Margaret said. This had become the pattern. Jason and Margaret would argue, and he would leave. Sometimes for days. She went on to tell Miriam how unfair Jason was, how sensitive she was to his needs, and that if he would change just a little bit, they could have a great relationship. Miriam's response was always the same, though worded differently each time.

One of the first things Miriam did after becoming a Christian was move out of the apartment she had been sharing with her boyfriend. Nobody told her she had to do that, but she felt it was the right thing to do. It was like an inner voice or conviction that living together outside of marriage was wrong. A lot of people, even some in the church, criticized her for this decision. She had established a regular practice of spending time in prayer and Scripture study. It was during one of those times of study she came to learn that she had been right all along. As it turned out, the things she feared would happen never happened. God took care of finding her a nicer place, and for lower rent!

So, on this day, Miriam was counseling her friend. "Margie, you know I love you. You're the sister I never had. But you know I won't lie to you, either." Miriam was trying to find a way to say what she always said when Margaret complained about Jason. "God is waiting for you to turn away from Jason, to turn toward Him. Jason cannot fill the void in your heart; only God can. Just look at your history. Every man you've ever linked up with has been a broken person you tried to fix. First, they didn't want to be fixed. And second, you are not the fixer. Even a blind person can see that they all fit the pattern of people who want to live life their way. They choose to be their own god. And guess what? You are not any different. You think you can fix someone when it's you who needs fixing as much as them. You can't fix you, and I can't fix you, but I can point you to one who can."

"Who is that?" Margaret had never experienced Miriam—or anybody—speaking to her like this. She wanted to tell her where to get off, but she felt strangely drawn to these words as well.

"Jesus." Miriam paused to let the name sink in. She was silently praying that the Holy Spirit would open Margaret's eyes to her real need.

"Jesus? That's all?"

"Well, uh, yeah."

"You have to be kidding," was Margaret's initial response. "You make it sound like Jesus is some kind of magic pill. I quit believing in magic a long time ago." Margaret didn't know it, but Miriam recognized that this was a smoke screen, one intended by the enemy to get them off track. Miriam knew enough not to take the bait.

"Margie, you've been trying to run your own life, and look where it's gotten you. You're not a bad person, but are you really happy? Do you ever wonder if this is all there is to life?" Miriam was hoping to appeal to Margaret's desire to have real meaning in her life. She remembered earlier conversations in which the two of them would discuss not only the meaning of life in general, but the purpose of their lives in particular. "You have a purpose, but you will never discover it until you come to know who gave you that purpose," Miriam said.

"Oh, Miriam, I just don't know." Margaret was starting to tear up. It wasn't long before the tears flowed down her cheeks, wetting the tablecloth her grandmother had given her. "I'm so scared. Jason has been staying away longer and longer. I half expect to hear someday that he has been hurt—or worse."

"Sweetheart, you can't save Jason. We are all responsible for our own decisions, and if you continue down this road, you will end up at the same place as Jason." Miriam paused. "You really have to turn to God and away from Jason. Only Jesus can fill the void we have in our lives."

"How do I do that?"

Miriam thought she'd never ask. Miriam gently took her through understanding that everyone, including her, had fallen short, that all are by nature rebellious against God. "We call that sin," Miriam said. "We are all sinners." Then she explained how God's holiness required that a sacrifice be made to pay the penalty for sin, and that's where Jesus came in. He was the sacrifice. He is referred to as the Lamb who takes away the sin of the world. God loved Margaret so much, Miriam said, that He gave his only Son, Jesus, to die on a cruel cross so the relationship between her and God could be put back together again.

A light seemed to go on in Margaret's mind. If what Miriam was saying was true, then that meant there was still hope for her. And it meant that Christianity was not about a list of do's and don'ts. It was not about hating those who were different. It actually leveled the playing field. If we are all sinners and separated from God, and if He sacrificed his only son to pay the price for our sins, this was more than a *religion*. It was about having a personal relationship with the God who created Margaret and gave her purpose. She almost missed the rest of what Miriam said as she came to grips with the love God had for her and anyone else who believed.

"Margie! Margie! Are you there?" Miriam chuckled, and her words brought Margaret back to the present. Miriam went on to tell her that she needed to confess her sins, accept Jesus as her Savior, and confess that He is Lord. Margaret was already there. Whether this happened in the sequence that Miriam said she was not sure, but there was one thing of which Margaret was certain. A few minutes before, she had been desperate for relief and despondent about life, and now it was like a tsunami of love had washed over her. She had never felt such peace, and there was a lightness about her. She was to learn later that everyone's salvation experiences are different. Some feel nothing. Some see visions. Some receive revelations. Maybe it was God giving to each person what they needed in the moment. Whatever it was, Margaret felt as though she had been taken to another dimension. The love she felt she had never received seemed to be given to her many times over. It came upon her in waves, one after another, and felt like warm liquid silk.

She cried tears of joy, and when she could focus her eyes a bit, she saw Miriam was smiling and crying right along with her. She had never felt anything like it, and in her mind's eye, she thought she saw God smiling.

SIX

Life Paths

Jack and Jason had grown closer during the months they worked at the warehouse. They partied a bit much, and Jack in particular found himself spending too much money. It seemed Jason usually didn't have his wallet with him or didn't have enough money whenever any significant expense came up. Jason always promised to pay Jack back, but Jack never saw any of that money.

Both Jack and Jason had big plans. Jack's original thought about going to college on his dime was still on his mind, but it was now sinking lower and lower on his priority list. Jason wasn't interested in anything to do with schooling. He couldn't go to college anyway. He had dropped out of school in tenth grade and never received a GED. He didn't like to be told what to do. He didn't like sitting in a class and listening to a boring lecture by a boring teacher who probably never had any fun in life, who was only there because he couldn't do anything else. At least that's how Jason saw it. There was nothing in school, he figured, that he couldn't learn on his own.

Indeed, Jason was learning a lot—just all the wrong things. He was learning that work was hard, and he didn't like it. When he saw how much money was being taken out in taxes, and how small his paycheck was, he was sure he was being cheated. "It's just like the government to screw the little guy," Jason would complain to whoever would listen. "Look at this. Almost half my paycheck is going to keep some bureaucrat fat and happy in a cushy office somewhere doing a do-nothing job." Jason was going to be somebody someday, and no one was going to take advantage of him.

Jack was just as ambitious, but not quite as vocal. He didn't always think before he spoke, but for the most part, he knew when to speak and when to keep quiet. Nonetheless, his reasoning went along the same lines as Jason's. He was determined to make something of himself. He too had noticed how people were looked down upon if they didn't have a title or money. Well, he didn't have a title, and he didn't have money, but he was going to have money whether he got a title or not. Titles are misleading, Jack thought. Sure, in some places, you get a title, and maybe a little better office, but they still treat you like a dog. Middle management was still slavery as far as he saw it. Worse, the workers don't like you, and you have to kiss up to senior management. You're caught in the middle. The worst of both worlds. No, Jack was going to be somebody on his terms.

In the meantime, Jason was moving ahead with his own plans. He got together with some of his old acquaintances and went back to doing what he had been doing before, fencing stolen property and dabbling in drugs. The only reason he was working at the warehouse was to expand his connections and get some extra money to buy more drugs. That was why he never seemed to have spending money when he was with Jack. He was shoveling every penny he could into buying more drugs. The market was ripe for the taking, and he saw this as an opportunity to reach his goal of becoming filthy rich.

They reached the point in which he confided to Jack about what he was doing and convinced him to join. He described it as both an adventure and an easy way to make money. This appealed to Jack. He too was tired of working for peanuts and then giving half of it to the government. For Jack, this also was a way of getting back at the government because he would not be paying any taxes on his "earnings." Anyway, the job at the warehouse was coming to an end, and he needed to find another way to make money. This opportunity came at just the right time. Luck was finally on Jack Olsen's side.

Jack had a terrible time with algebra and geometry back in high school. Everyone insisted that he take those classes so he could go to college. Big fat help that was. All it did was bring his grade point average down so that, even if he wanted to go to college, he would have a hard time finding one that would accept him no matter what Mr. Simpson said. It also made him dislike traditional learning, and in this he was a lot like Jason. Too many people in his life telling him what to do, expectations set so high that he could never reach them. It made him what he had become: an untrusting, uneducated, insecure, angry, and scared young man. That was why he hit it off so well with Jason. As they say: "Birds of a feather flock together."

However, there was one thing Jack did discover he was pretty good at that Jason wasn't: simple adding and subtracting. This worked to bring them more together in "business."

Jason had the contacts. He knew who dealt in what drugs, and he knew where and when he could get them. He had been living in the area for most of his life since his father left the family high and dry. It was only natural that he would return there after his time in prison. He carved himself a nice slice of the drug trade in the area, and Jason began to expand into outlying communities. Jack kept the books. He knew where each penny went. He paid off those who needed to be paid off, and he made sure that Jason and he got the lion's share of the profits. Indeed, Jack thought, his dreams were starting to come to pass.

Meanwhile, Margaret and Jason's relationship continued to go downhill. He was not paying his way, and Margaret had to pick up the slack. The more money he made dealing drugs and fencing stolen property, the less he pitched in at home. She didn't know about his criminal activities. As far as she was concerned, he was working at the warehouse. He never told her it was seasonal work, so she didn't even notice when it was done. As it was, he was making more money now than he ever had before, so she really had no reason to suspect anything. She just wished he would contribute more around the apartment.

She had other thoughts bothering her. Since she accepted Christ, Margaret had a continuing feeling that living with Jason was wrong. It was more than a nagging feeling. It felt like she was being convicted on the inside. She had learned enough about being a follower of Christ that she wondered if this was the Holy Spirit trying to tell her something. All Miriam would tell her was her experience with her boyfriend, that when she finally left the apartment they shared, her life took on an added dimension of blessings. Her thinking became clearer, and her decisions increasingly became the right ones, Miriam said. Not to say that she still didn't make bad ones at times, but it seemed that doors opened for her that she had not noticed before.

Miriam encouraged Margaret to learn to pray about things. At first, she was uncomfortable with the idea. After all, talking when no one was in the room with you was what crazy people did, wasn't it? "I only do what the voices in my head tell me to do" was a joke she had heard many times. So, wasn't praying too close to listening to the voices in one's head? Not only that, but wasn't there some special religious language or tone that one was supposed to use when addressing God? All of these confusing thoughts kept her from praying, and it looked like she was going to quit her Christian walk.

It was a good thing that Miriam prayed. Some would probably describe her as a prayer warrior. She would not give up on Margaret. Not only would she pray, she gently nudged her friend toward God.

"Maggie, I've told you about how God worked with me when I was living with Brad. He convicted me that it was wrong, that if I was going to follow him, I would need to lay down some things of this world, and living with Brad was one of them."

"But I love Jason. I know he can change if I stay with him."

"God loves Jason too, but it's not up to you to change him," Miriam said. "He will make his own decisions, and God will deal with him when Jason is ready. Look, Maggie, I won't tell you that you must leave him, but I will tell you to seek God about this. I don't want you to leave Jason because I say so. I want you to do what God says because you love God more than anything in the world. Remember the love you felt when you accepted Christ? There is nothing you can do to earn it. Remember how you loved Him back? Well, love is more than a feeling. It is shown by actions. We love Him because He first loved us, but we show it by our behavior, by our obedience to what He says. It's easier to obey when you are motivated by love.

"I do think you are complicating prayer too much. It's simply talking to God just like you talk to a friend. You don't use a bunch of pious-sounding words when you and I talk, do you? It's the same way with God. Tell Him what you're thinking, what you're feeling. If you are angry, tell Him. If you are sad, tell Him. You are not hiding anything that he doesn't already know. What you will find is that He will honor your honesty and bring peace to your heart that passes understanding. A lot of the things you worry about will simply vanish, and He will give you wisdom and understanding on how to deal with the challenges you face. It is the most liberating thing."

Miriam was making a lot of sense. Margaret would have to consider her words, and who knows, she thought, she might even pray in the way Miriam was talking about. For now, it would have to suffice to slow down with Jason.

* * * * *

Jason came home, late as usual, one night. Margaret tried to make him feel at home. She brought him a beer and asked if he would like something to eat. Late as it was, she was willing to serve him, as that was part of who she was. At heart, she liked to serve, and she still had hopes that Jason and she would develop into something permanent. She also hoped that the saying "the way to a man's heart is through his stomach" was true.

But Jason had his mind elsewhere. Margaret could tell. Sometimes he would come home not only tired but angry. She could never understand where the anger was coming from, but she had quit wondering if she was the source of it. She wasn't perfect, she knew, but Jason's anger was erratic and unpredictable enough that she figured it couldn't all be related to her.

When a person has unresolved issues, anger is usually not far behind. Jason's anger came from a lifetime of rejection and unmet expectations. He was unable to let things go, to leave the past behind. Once in a while, he would explode in a fit of anger over all the perceived injustices he had experienced. He could name names and places. Forgiveness was not something Jason practiced much. But he did insist on justice. That is, he wanted justice for those who had hurt him in some way. When it came to the wrongs he had done, however, he wanted mercy for himself. At the very least, he wanted people to understand why he did the things he did, and then they would realize he was justified in his behavior.

This night, he was especially distracted. His drug business was growing, Jack was keeping good numbers, and he was beginning to think they might have to bring another person in the inner circle. But his biggest concern was Margaret. He truly did like her, but she had started to get religious, and that just would not do. He had no time for some fairy in the sky. To add to his confusion, she was not reacting to him as before. She did not snap at him or call him names or complain as much. Something was going on with her, and he hated that he could not figure it out. There was a time when he thought they would live happily ever after, but now he wasn't so sure. Why can't people remain the same? It was a lot easier when he thought he understood her.

Jason spent considerable mental energy that night thinking about how he would get even with those who had wronged him in the past. He also thought a lot about Margaret and what was to become of their future. He really could not get a handle on anything. His mind just swirled around possible scenarios and questions. Then the phone rang.

"Jason, are you still awake?" It was Jack. Jack rarely called this late unless something was up.

"Jack? What's up, man? I was just thinking about you."

"Listen, we may have a problem with Mikey. No, we *do* have a problem with Mikey. I thought about calling you tomorrow, but I thought you would want to know about this right away."

"Get to the point. What's up with Mikey?"

Mikey was one of Jason's old buddies he had linked up with when he got out of prison. Mikey knew people, and he introduced Jason to them. In fact, if it hadn't been for Mikey, Jason would not have been able to build his business. Mikey had all the contacts, but he didn't have Jason's drive. Over time, it became obvious that Jason was the leader. Jack, by virtue of his skill with numbers and steady thinking, also bypassed Mikey in importance within the organization. There was also a quiet distrust and competition between Mikey and Jack.

Mikey had a good piece of the business. Jason allocated the southwestern part of the state to him, so that meant he also got northern Indiana and even a part of Illinois. It was his to build, and as long as Jason got his cut of the profits, life was good.

Mikey always had a sense of feeling cheated, no matter how good the deal was for him. After all, it was his contacts that made Jason who he was, and, by extension, Mikey would argue that he made Jack who he was as well. It seemed unfair that Jason was now the boss, and, from Mikey's perspective, he had become just another employee. Jack had always suspected that Mikey would eventually make a move to push Jason aside, but he could not voice his suspicions without seeming to initiate a turf battle. Jack knew Jason trusted his judgment, but he did not want to spend that trust on stirring up things that may or may not be true. What happened a few nights ago, and was going to happen again tonight, was enough to compel him to call Jason.

Mikey had indeed built up the business in the southwestern part of Michigan, and into parts of two other states. But also, like Jason, he had scrimped and saved from his earnings so that he was able to buy product for himself. Instead of funneling all the new business to Jason's empire, he gave enough to Jason to keep up the image of growth, while at the same time building his own network of sellers and buyers. To make things worse, he was not stopping his network from expanding to the east, so Jason was finding himself competing against distributors who were loyal to Mikey. Jason's business, ever so slowly, was beginning to shrink.

Jack learned about this by mistake. Mikey had Jack's number, and he accidentally gave it to one of his distributors, who called the number, thinking it was Mikey's private number. The distributor left a voice message for Mikey telling him of the previous night's drug purchase and the upcoming deal that night. Jack thought it was a normal business transaction, that the caller had simply made a mistake. No harm, no foul. That is, until he got toward the end of the message, when the caller made it clear that Jason would not know about any of the ongoing deals and their plans to move their business to the east.

Jason was not pleased in the least. His mind immediately linked this latest betrayal to the long list of perceived betrayals he had suffered in the past. He went over them as though he had been transported back in time and was experiencing them again and again. His head was a mixture of anger and sadness. He was speechless for a moment, and it wasn't until Jack asked Jason what he wanted to do that the head man came back to the present.

"Is George still in town?" Jason asked. George was a mid-level dealer hoping to move up in the organization. He was supposed to travel to California, but Jason couldn't remember when. Jason recalled hearing George brag about the time he spent as a sniper in the military. Jason was thinking George could put those skills to work and put himself in a concealed position near the drug deal, take pictures, and then they would have all the evidence they needed to confront Mikey. Jack replied that he didn't know if George was around, but he would check and get back with him.

It took Jack longer than he hoped to contact George. George had a habit of being hard to find. He had a personal philosophy that he didn't want to be found; instead, he wanted to be able to find you when he wanted something. And this was a key factor why he wasn't rising faster in the business. When there were windows of opportunity, George couldn't be found—until the windows had shut.

It was getting dark when Jack and George met up. Jason had told Jack to work it out with George, and to let him know later how things went. Jack met George at a pancake house, and as they sipped on coffee and picked at some pancakes and hash browns, Jack filled George in on the details and what Jason expected. You could see George getting excited about the possibilities. He hadn't used his sniper skills to sneak up on anyone since his time in Afghanistan. The last time, although he accomplished his mission, he barely got away with his life. Granted, he wasn't going to kill anyone this time, but a lot of things could go wrong. There was no telling what would happen to him if he was discovered.

Time was getting away, so George and Jack headed to Jack's place for a quick how-to on the camera. The camera was specially fitted to take pictures in low light without needing a flash. The idea was to position close enough to get the type of pictures that would identify the people making the exchange. Jack also hoped George would get enough additional images to show where the event was happening and the money and drugs being exchanged. Jason wanted George to provide enough details so he would have plenty of options. He might want to just threaten Mikey, or he might go as far as killing him, making an example of him to others who might be thinking of similar paths. Jason had never killed anyone before, but people who knew him suspected he had ordered hits in the past. Jason certainly gave the impression that he was capable. As far as he was concerned, the image was as good as the reality for controlling people.

The meeting was to take place in the warehouse district. Lots of money flowed through the businesses associated with this district. Most were legitimate, some were fronts. As with most warehouse concentrations in most cities, some of the buildings were empty. Some were in such disrepair that the homeless had made themselves comfortable there. It was not a safe area to be around at night. The daytime would reveal the remains of drug paraphernalia and cast-off clothes that seemed to appear out of nowhere. On this particular night, the only light came from one lamppost. The other lights had either gone out on a timer, burned out, or been taken out by someone playing some sort of thoughtless game of seeing how many times throwing rocks it would take to hit and break the bulbs. It was also a moonless night. This was the kind of opportunity that the lowlifes—the underbellies—of society would use to try to get around the norms of civilized living.

Mikey had his own crew, and he trusted them to set up the meeting. This was the way he had learned from Jason. Everything worked well for him. Little did Mikey know that his oft-repeated adage, the one he said he lived by—"there is no trust among thieves"—was about to come back and bite him.

Usually, Mikey sent one or two of his crew to make the purchase or sale. This time would be different in that he was going to be there in person. The buyer was an ambitious guy who wanted to expand his territory and was willing to give a piece of the action to Mikey. Mikey wanted to do this deal himself; this was too big to leave to a subordinate. In addition, it could pay off big for Mikey because, not only would he get a piece of the action by continuing to expand his own territory to the east, he would be sure to meet other dealers who could use his services. This could mushroom into something big—big enough that Jason would not be able to stop it even if he wanted to.

If Jack and George could get good pictures of the deal going down, as they wanted, Jason would have all he needed to trap Mikey.

Greed. It's what's for dinner. If greed was the entree, insecurity was the appetizer, with fear and pride serving as nice side dishes. Like many people, Mikey dreamed of greatness for himself. He came from a family that used fear to keep everyone in line. There was the fear of failure, but also the fear of being different. A herd mentality guided the beliefs and actions of everyone in the organization. But Mikey always resisted the pressure to conform to the herd. He wanted to succeed more than he feared failure. He had natural abilities, but he didn't understand, or he chose to ignore, his blind spots. Greed and pride would eventually lead to his downfall. Here he was, experiencing success in his line of work—illegal as it was—and instead of being satisfied, he allowed greed to overcome him. Now he would pay a heavy price.

Just not on this night.

* * * * *

George had learned from an informant in Jack's network when and where the meeting was taking place, so he was already in position when the main players began to show up. There had been some doubt whether Mikey would make an appearance. His name was never mentioned in the email traffic or phone calls Jason and Jack's guys hacked into. They finally discovered Mikey had been given a nickname, "The Great White," as in "The Great White Shark." This was a comical reference to an Asian great white shark. This could only mean Mikey, because he came from Asian roots, and his physical features were Asian. However, Mikey couldn't speak anything but inner-city English, and if you heard him on the phone, you might think he was anything but Asian.

"Georgie, are you there?"

George and Jack were using their phones to stay in touch through the evening. Jack didn't think Mikey's operation was sophisticated enough to hack into their phones, so they felt confident enough to use them without taking any protective measures. From his vantage point, George kept his voice extremely low, but was audible enough for Jack to hear him.

"Don't call me Georgie, Jackie."

Even in dangerous times, George and Jack could not keep from playing around. Never mind that if George was discovered, it could cost him his life.

"Do you see anything?"

"No, but I can tell you it's getting cold up here. Being inside a building isn't much help in the heating department when all the windows are broken and the wind is blowing through here like it owns the place."

"It's not going to get any warmer," Jack said. "Hope they show up soon. I hate it when you whine about a little runny nose."

"Remind me to break yours when I see you again."

On and on they went, each trying to outdo the other with boyish machismo when, all of a sudden, George turned very serious.

"Hold on. Something is happening." George noticed some dimmed car lights in the distance. It was obvious someone was trying to approach the area without drawing too much attention to themselves.

It was a little early, but maybe Mikey or the buyer were trying to get in the best position in case this deal went south.

"What do you see? Don't keep me hanging."

"Shut up. All I see is a slow-moving vehicle with parking lights on." It reminded George of field training during his days in the Army. They would drive in the dark practicing what was called light discipline. They would try to avoid being detected by driving with just parking lights on. He wondered if he was facing some guys with military training. He also began to wonder if being there by himself without backup was such a good idea.

"How many are there?"

"Stand by."

It seemed like an eternity. The car eventually came to a stop behind a Dumpster, and the driver cut the lights. A few minutes later, another car came into view. This one was moving a little more briskly. It drove directly toward the parked car.

"Holy . . ."

"What happened? What's going on?" You could hear anxiety rising in Jack's voice.

"You're not going to believe this."

"Believe *what!?* Are you getting the pictures?"

"Oh yeah, I'm getting pictures. But it's not what you expected." Jack thought he could almost hear a chuckle in George's response.

The first car, it turned out, contained a teenage couple who had just been looking for a place to make out. They were sure they had found the perfect spot when the second car came upon them and suddenly turned on its bright lights and siren. Two undercover policemen jumped out, guns pointed at the young couple. They shouted several times for them to get out of the car and drop to the ground. In the next few minutes, George was able to make out that the policemen thought they had come upon a drug deal of some kind. George couldn't help but laugh at the thought of how the young couple were going to explain all this to their parents. (Would the young man dare try to use the old "ran out of gas" excuse, or would he say they got lost on the way home? Would they say the police were harassing them? The possibilities might be endless, but also nearly impossible to pull off.)

The police would have at least two things to handle with this. One would be the amount of paperwork they would have to file reporting this event and their role in it. The second would be the inevitable joking they would have to endure from their fellow officers when word got out that they had busted a couple of teenagers trying to express their young love.

George was doing all he could to keep from laughing loud enough to be heard by the people below. He also wanted to get the pictures because he knew no one was going to believe him otherwise.

Meanwhile, where was "The Great White" and the ambitious drug buyer? Had their plan of mutual enrichment been interrupted by what had just taken place? Perhaps the intel was wrong. Maybe they were meeting somewhere else at that very moment; maybe Jack's info had been bad. George waited for a few more hours until he was sure nothing else was going to happen that night. Unceremoniously, in the wee hours of the morning, he left for home.

Meanwhile, Jack stayed up the rest of the night trying to figure out what happened—and how he was going to explain it to Jason.

SEVEN

Ripples

Susan had made clear to Jack that she would be going to college close to home. She did not get into her school of first choice, however, and she had come to terms with the fact that she would have to live in a women's dorm or get an apartment during the school year. She had hoped to live at home with her parents to save money, but having to go to her second choice for college required her to limit her time at home to holidays and when her job allowed time off. With all this on the table, before Jack left home to move to the promised land of Detroit, he gave Susan an ultimatum. He was moving to Detroit according to plan, and if she wanted their relationship to continue, she would either come with him or join him there in a week.

As much as she wanted to be with him, she knew she would not make that choice. Unlike Jack, she had a sense of what it meant to pack up and move so far away from family and friends. She didn't like the idea that her college was as far away as it was, and that was only a half day's travel from home. There was also the problem of where she would live once she got there. She and Jack had not been intimate, as so many of their friends had. Although tempted, she was determined to save herself for the right man, the man God would send to her. As far as she was concerned, that meant marriage. Jack had not mentioned the living arrangements, but she felt he was expecting her to move in with him—and that was just not going to happen.

If Jack was thinking along such lines, he never let on, and from his actions, it seemed his mind was preoccupied with the unexpected issues he encountered when he got to Detroit. His job and housing did not materialize as he expected, he soon found himself involved in criminal activity, and he had developed a paranoia that he did not have before. He certainly hadn't expected his initial foray away from the security of his family to develop like this. As it was, there was a certain excitement in what he was doing. He knew he could go to jail, even prison, and he knew the people he was running with were not the most stable. Jason was becoming more unstable every day, and Jack was looking forward to the day when he could split off and start his own business. Because of all this, his relationship with Susan was over. He was meeting other girls who were more adventuresome than her anyway.

Meanwhile, Susan was not standing still. Her life was full of activities. She had found a church to attend. Her academic schedule was full, and she had taken on the part-time job to make ends meet, as she expected. She didn't want to ask her parents for anything if she could help it. They would help her for sure, but she wanted to prove she could be on her own. Little did she know that they worried about her constantly and prayed for her all the time. Not because they didn't trust her, but because she was their little girl, the firstborn and first of their children to leave home.

She was meeting new people at college and being exposed to new ideas. Her faith kept her anchored, so she didn't stray far from the values she brought from home. She remembered what her father told her before she left: "You will make friends who are the same kinds of friends you had here. You will also meet people from very different backgrounds and beliefs. Those people will challenge everything you have ever been taught, and you will have to decide for yourself what you will allow in your life. I wish we could be there to hold your hand and keep you from making mistakes, but we have done our best to give you a good foundation to face the world. You will make mistakes, but that will just remind you that you are human. Remember where you came from, remember your God, live accordingly, learn from your mistakes, and things will turn out just fine."

Meanwhile, Jack's family was going through its own struggles with Jack's absence. Fatherhood was not meant to be this difficult. Jack's father had raised Jack in a family that believed in the proverbial Puritan work ethic. "Early to bed, early to rise, makes a man healthy, wealthy, and wise." "The early bird gets the worm." These were sayings—whether they originated with Benjamin Franklin centuries ago, or whoever—that were common in Jack's childhood. Another one Jack remembered clearly was, "a penny saved is a penny earned." As a result, he learned to work harder than most, and some of his friends called him stingy for his refusal to spend hard-earned money on things that weren't important. With all these teachings in mind, it wasn't that Jack's father wasn't generous. He was quick to give to charity and to those who needed a helping hand.

Another thing Jack learned early on was to respect his elders. He didn't remember if he was ever guilty of being disrespectful. He did remember hearing a Bible verse in church about honoring your parents. Maybe that was what moved him to behave toward his parents the way he did. Even in the times he disagreed with them, he tried his hardest to do so respectfully. Of course, that meant he sometimes had to bite his lip to keep from saying something out of line, and he wasn't always successful at it. But his heart was in the right place; he was quick to apologize when he messed up.

So what happened to the Olsens' oldest son? It had been more than a year since Jack left home—way too early and unprepared, if you asked his dad. His departure was cordial, and there had been the usual exchanges of spoken and physical affection when a child leaves the nest. For his mother, it had been nearly as traumatic as when she put him on the bus for his first day of school.

They had agreed that Jack would call his mother at least monthly, and call them if he ever needed anything. Jack's dad didn't want to coddle his son, but both he and his wife agreed that Jack could struggle by himself with the difficulties of being on his own up until he needed money to eat or a roof over his head. For many months now, they had not heard that he needed such help, but neither had he kept his promise to call his mom every month. It caused them concern, and they worried that things weren't turning out like Jack had hoped.

Mom wrestled with her own thoughts. There was a side to Jack's mother that wanted to trust and believe others. It was a sort of naïveté that actually helped her get through what others would view as uncertain times. This time, however, was different. She sensed that things were not going according to Jack's plans. She had hoped he would call her every month, but wasn't really expecting him to do it since she knew how he was when he was at home. Sometimes his promises would go unfulfilled. But this was different. She hadn't heard from him in several months, and when she tried to contact him, he did not return her calls.

When she tried to talk with Jack's dad about her concerns, he would do what most husbands do: try to comfort her by making light of the situation. He insisted that Jack was just growing up. Jack was just experiencing the university of life, as he called it, adding that she shouldn't worry; Jack would be fine.

More than once, his mother spoke of taking a trip to Detroit to see how Jack was really doing. Each time, they agreed to let Jack reach out to them if he needed help. They had done the best they could in raising him.

Unknown to the both of them, of course, was just how precarious Jack's life had become. He found himself balancing between staying one step ahead of the law and navigating through the politics of the life of crime in which he found himself. He was not always successful. Early on, he had been picked up by police for suspicion of dealing drugs. They were right, of course, but didn't have solid proof. From then on, his paranoia kept him looking over his shoulder, and he became increasingly suspicious of unknown cars parking near where he lived. Several times, he came dangerously close to getting involved in fights he was ill-prepared to engage in. He became convinced he could trust no one.

Mom and Dad weren't the only ones concerned. Jack's brother and sister, Don and Becky, also were worried about him, though they tried to hide it. Becky kept herself busy at school with classes and activities. She was trying to decide if she wanted to try out for the cheerleading squad or join the yearbook club. She had always been interested in journalism, and others advised her that working on the yearbook would give her a taste of what that field is like. But cheerleading seemed like so much fun. As Becky wrestled with the challenges of growing up and preparing for her future, she thought and prayed for Jack—daily. Don was still at home as well, so he could see the dynamics of his parents' relationship as they tried to encourage each other and project a strong face for him and Becky. But they could only fake it for so long. Jack's absence was especially hard on Thanksgiving, when all of them were together—except for their eldest child.

This was actually the second year that all of them were not together. Mom made the same amount of food as every previous year, however. She even set a plate where Jack would sit if he were home. This was supposed to be a time of thanksgiving and rejoicing in what God had done for and through them, but there was a sadness too. There was not as much laughter, and the stories that were told lacked some of the enthusiasm of other years. At the meal, eventually, Don brought up the elephant in the room.

"What do you think Jack is doing right about now?"

Before the silence became overwhelming, Becky responded. "He is probably stuffing himself, and crawling somewhere to sleep it off, even as he tries to watch the football games."

That got a few smiles as they remembered that, each year, Jack would set a pillow on the living room floor and have a blanket nearby in case he got cold. His big plan was to eat the Thanksgiving meal, then stretch out on the floor and watch the Detroit Lions, hoping against hope they would finally win a game on Thanksgiving. More often than not, he would be disappointed, but it didn't matter. He rarely lasted more than fifteen minutes before he was asleep anyway. Every year after the Thanksgiving meal, Jack got some of the best sleep of his life on the living room floor.

What none of them knew was that, at the moment they were having this discussion, Jack was at a rescue mission. Of his few friends in Detroit, all had other plans for the day, so he had no one with whom to share the day and a big meal. He remembered that the mission had a free meal, so he made his way there and ate a decent meal, although, of course, it wasn't like home. He missed his mother's cooking.

Back home, Don's perspective on what he saw with his father was important. He looked up to his dad. He always had. His father had showed him how to hunt and fish, and he even knew a thing or two about computers and social media. When he heard his friends talk about how they had to help their parents figure out their phones, Don smiled with the knowledge that he never had to help his father. He seemed to always know new stuff.

But as Don looked at his dad now, on this day, he could see that the wrinkles of aging were getting more noticeable. Could it be that his dad was thinking of the empty chair at the table? Sometimes Dad kept things to himself. Don assumed it was to protect the family from unnecessary worries. Don wondered if there really was something to worry about.

EIGHT

Light Probes Darkness

A voicemail from Willy? Wow. Jack had not heard from Willy in more than a year. Last he knew, Willy was on the verge of dropping out of college, he was nowhere near taking over his father's business, and word on the street was that he had started to dabble in drugs. Maybe this call would be an opportunity for Jack to recruit him into his network.

"Hey, Willy! How have you been? Long time no see."

"A lot has happened," Willy began. "Thanks for returning my call. It would be cool to get together and do some catching up. When do you get off work?"

Jack wasn't about to tell Willy he had flexible hours—*very* flexible hours. Next thing you know, Willy would be asking questions Jack wasn't ready to answer.

"I'm going to have some time off next week," Jack said. "When do you want to meet up?"

"I'm going to have to check with the manager. I have a part-time job at a restaurant, and the schedule has already been set for the rest of the month, but I may be able to trade shifts or work something out. I'll get back to you."

"Whoa! A restaurant? Are you waiting tables? I thought you were going to take over your father's business?"

"That's a long story I can tell you about when we meet. I guess it's enough to say that man makes plans, but God directs his steps."

Whaa? Jack thought. *What was that all about?* Jack vaguely remembered that saying from somewhere, but he couldn't remember where or when. And that was the first time he ever heard Willy mention God in a sentence without using the name as a curse word. Jack didn't give it much thought in the moment, though, because he knew Willy like the back of his hand. What he didn't know was that a seed had been planted. Jack would later realize that he had heard the words, and let them hit him for a second, but he really hadn't been listening.

"OK, man. Call me when your schedule opens up. I'll work mine around yours."

Willy did not sound as nervous and full of himself as Jack remembered. *Oh well. People change,* Jack reasoned. In the back of his mind, though, Jack had a sense that there was more to this story than just that.

Jack had to rush to the other side of town to take care of business matters. He was carrying quite a bit of cash in his car to pay off a dealer. His mind was somewhere else when he drove up to a stop sign. He almost went through it without stopping. He stopped at the last second, his phone flying to the floor from the passenger side. Holding his stopped position, he reached down and picked it up. Good for him that the phone fell on the floor. Just as he was starting to edge into the intersection, a truck drove through the stop sign on his right, smashing into a car that had already entered the intersection opposite Jack. With Jack's heartbeat racing, he continued with his right turn, in the direction from which the truck had come. He couldn't afford to stay there and go through a bunch of questions from police. He could only hope that no one was hurt too badly. And so, Jack drove away from the scene. Later, he would think about the right and wrong of this decision not to stay and give help. But only for a minute or two. He thought more about how, as Jack saw it, he seemed to lead a charmed life. He had missed serious injury or death several times, sometimes by seconds, just like what happened at that stop sign. It was like it wasn't his time to die. He just was a lucky guy, he figured.

* * * * *

Jack and Willy met a few weeks later, and after a quick hug and commenting on each other's appearance, they reminisced about old times. It wasn't long before Jack heard Willy apologizing.

"Hey, man, I am sorry for how things unfolded when you came to town. I knew months ahead of your getting here that there wouldn't be a job waiting for you, and that I would need to move back in with my parents. I was just unwilling to face the facts, and you ended up getting hurt."

Jack couldn't believe his ears. Was this the same Willy who wouldn't admit to any weakness? The same Willy who used to brag about his future? Jack was not used to hearing apologies from anyone, so he stumbled as he let Willy know, in his own way, that it was OK. He switched the subject.

"How are your parents? When I was there, your mom didn't like me, and was all wrapped up in her artwork. Has she gotten rich and famous yet?"

"Neither rich or famous. But she's the happiest I've ever seen her. Her artwork has become more well known, and she is making more money. In fact, if my dad quit working today, she could probably support the family with what she makes. But that is not what makes her happy. She has taken her newfound celebrity—well, sort of, local celebrity anyway—and is blessing others. By that I mean she gives most of her money away."

"Hold on. Say what? That doesn't make any sense."

"That's not all. My father's business is booming. He's got enough work to keep him busy for years to come. And remember, we live in one of the most depressed cities in the country."

"I think you're messing with me. You're making my head spin. There's got to be a reason for all this."

"Jack, you've known me a long time, since back in our days in school together. And you lived at my house long enough to see how we really are. Would it surprise you to know I can pinpoint the reason for the change that's happened to us?"

"OK, I'll bite. What's the reason for this change?"

"Jesus."

"Say what?"

"It's Jesus."

"What the—!" Jack practically spit out the words before stopping himself. "What do you mean by that?"

"It really started with my mom and an acquaintance of hers in the art world. They were sitting at a coffee shop, having their Starbucks, and her friend starts telling her about how she had come to know Jesus Christ."

"Wait a minute." Jack stopped the story. "You got *religion*?"

"No, no. Let me finish. I'll try to give you the short version. This lady told my mother that it was possible to know Jesus personally. Of course, that blew my mom away because it just sounded like some mumbo jumbo mystical thing. She told me later that she fully expected to be sold some book or incense. Totally weird."

"I would agree with that, for sure."

"But it wasn't that at all. This woman tells my mom that the Jesus of the Bible isn't as interested in religion as He is in having a personal relationship with people."

"Say that again."

"Sure. I said, Jesus is more interested in having a personal relationship than He is in religion."

"That's crazy! And impossible! I've been around religious people, and all I ever heard was, 'Do this. Don't do that.' There was always a sense that God was somehow standing over you with a big paddle waiting for you to mess up so he could smack you down. It was all a list of do's and don'ts, and it didn't matter if you knew the list, because it would change tomorrow. You just live hoping that you don't cross some line you can't see. It's impossible to live like that! That's why I ran away from that as soon and as far as I could."

Will remained calm. He paused for just a moment, then asked, "How's that working for you?"

"What do you mean? I'm as good as the next person. Sure, I have issues, but who doesn't?"

Before Jack could continue his near-rant about the uselessness of religion and hypocrisy in the church, Willy brought him back to his story.

"My mother reacted pretty much the same way at first. But she couldn't get away from the change that had taken place in her friend. She decided to search it out for herself. After all, if she was going to discuss religion, she was going to have to get smart herself. She figured that a short study of the Bible would be all she would need to debunk this personal relationship stuff."

"She failed, didn't she?"

"Well, yes. When she got into the Bible, she just got drawn in more and more. She hadn't given her friend enough time to tell her more. But she discovered, on her own, that the personal relationship thing was a result of something more important."

"What was that?"

"Repentance."

"What?"

"Repentance. That means changing your mind. It's like you're walking in one direction, and you change your mind and go in another direction."

"I guess I'm repenting every day, 'cause I change my mind about a lot of things," Jack said with a small laugh.

"No, no. That's not it. Mom discovered that she could not meet God's standard. She had broken God's laws, and that was the definition of a sinner."

"No one's perfect."

"Exactly! All of us have messed up and fallen short. She needed to agree with God about her condition, ask Him to forgive her, and to save her. She read a text that really affected her. It was Romans 10:9: 'If you declare with your mouth, Jesus is Lord, and believe in your heart that God raised him from the dead, you will be saved.' So that's what she did in prayer. It doesn't happen the same with everyone, but she started to experience some pretty dramatic changes in her life. And then Dad got on board, and I did—"

"Hold on." Jack jumped in. "I'm not buying what you're selling. This all sounds looney tunes to me. I'm as good as the next guy, and I've seen too much hatred and hypocrisy in this world, including the church, to believe that, all of a sudden, God can turn things around like flipping a switch. If this God exists, I would want to ask him why bad things happen to good people, and why he—supposedly a good

God—would allow all the bad stuff that happens, like natural disasters and terrorist attacks. This is a crock. Willy, I thought you were smarter than to fall for such fairy dust."

Will could see that he had hit a wall. Jack was not willing to hear anymore. He knew Jack was going through some things, but he didn't want to push too hard. For now, Will would have to be satisfied that he had planted some seed, and maybe Jack would allow it to take root in the future.

* * * * *

In the meantime, Jack had other things on his mind. His partnership with Jason was not going smoothly, and he had to work on that. Jack was certain that Mikey was undermining their business in the east, but he couldn't prove it. That one time he tried to get pictures of Mikey doing a rogue deal, all he got from his "sniper photographer," George, were shots of a teenage couple being surprised by police when they were making out in an isolated warehouse parking lot. And now, the person most responsible for Jack being in this city, the person who had made such empty promises in the beginning, who was at least partly to blame for the hard times he had encountered—this person had now found Jesus. What a waste.

By the time Jack got back to his side of town, it was dark. This was actually a good thing because he did his best work after dark. He decided to check in on Bobby and see if their numbers lined up.

Jack was responsible for keeping the numbers. He would make sure that the people downline got their share of the profits, but that he and Jason got the bigger slices. But he wasn't a real accountant. Bobby was a real accountant. Bobby even had a college degree. Jack suspected that Bobby was brought in to double-check his numbers. This wasn't, in itself, a bad idea, except that Jason had not told Jack that was the reason, so it made Jack think that Jason was beginning to suspect his friend going behind his back.

This was not good. Sure, Jack was hoping to one day either replace Jason or go out on his own. The first would be extremely dangerous; how the latter would be done had to be thought through carefully.

Jack had seen what happened to others who were less sensitive to Jason's eccentricities. He especially thought about Mikey. Jason had suspected him for some time. It seemed that Jason was losing share of whatever market touched on Mikey's assigned turf. This could only mean that someone in Mikey's organization—or Mikey himself—was dealing beyond the boundaries. Even though he slipped through Jack and George's great plan to catch him in the act with a camera, Mikey had, as the saying goes, been given enough rope to eventually hang himself.

* * * * *

It happened, of all times, when Jason, Jack, and some of the inner core of the organization were at Mikey's place for a barbecue. They didn't get a chance to get together like this often, but this was the middle of the week, the weather was good, and their busy time wouldn't hit until the weekend. And the smell of ribs and brisket made this afternoon all worthwhile.

Neither Jack nor the others were big drinkers, but Jason was. Of all his faults, drinking was near the top. Sometimes he would be a mean drunk; other times he would get depressed when drinking. One never knew which Jason was going to show up.

All the guys arrived about midafternoon. Mikey had already put the meat on the grill. He prided himself on the special rub he put on the meat. It was his secret recipe, and the other guys loved to kid him about it. They spent most of the afternoon telling stories on each other and harassing Mikey about his rub recipe. Of course, as the drinking increased, the stories got less believable. In all, they were having a good time, and they wouldn't know—until later—the significant change that took place on that day.

As the sun was going down, Jason had to take his umpteenth trip to Mikey's bathroom. You cannot drink a lot and not expect to have to go more often. The bathroom was next to the office that Mikey had rigged up in his house. Mikey liked to think of himself as a big businessman. In a way, he was, because his business was growing faster than anyone else's in the organization. That was part of the reason

Jason suspected Mikey was somehow cheating. Mikey was good, but not that good. To Jason and some of the others, something smelled—and more powerfully than the barbecue.

Jason insisted that all of his leaders be reachable at all times. Everyone, including Mikey, had smartphones. Anytime, day or night, they had their phones with them. And they kept them on—all, that is, except Mikey. Mikey did not sleep much, but when he did, he did not want to be disturbed. It wasn't the best idea, but he decided that to compensate for his not being completely available 24/7, he would put in a landline. That was an old-fashioned phone that could receive messages even if the power went out and the cell towers were not working. On that fateful day, the answering machine on his desk phone would betray him.

As Jason stumbled into the bathroom, he heard the phone ringing in the background. He didn't make any special effort to alert Mikey; he let the call roll into voice mail. What he heard next helped sober him up, and quickly.

"Hey, Mikey. This is Pete. That large shipment is coming in earlier than we expected this week. We need to find some place to store it before we can distribute it to our dealers. How do you want to handle it? Give me a call back when you get this. We don't have as much time as we thought."

This was the smoking gun. Jason didn't know who this Pete was, but he knew for certain that no shipment was scheduled for the next two weeks. This was proof positive that Mikey was undercutting him. When he went out to join the rest of the guys, his depressed persona showed up. Jack noticed the change, but he wasn't sure anyone else did. They were all pretty much drunk by then.

The party broke up sooner than usual. To his credit, Jason did not bring up what he heard on the answering machine. But he did ask Jack and Bobby to meet him later that night at one of their secret meeting spots. Jack found this a bit unusual. They normally met at a small office they had leased some time back. For some reason, Jason did not want to meet there. The secret places were usually reserved for immediate crises or problems that needed to be dealt with right away. Jack was not aware of anything that was so critical it required an immediate meeting. And if it was so important, why didn't Jason invite more of the key leadership? This all seemed very strange to him.

Jason had sobered up some, but his speech was still slurred, and his thought process certainly wasn't one hundred percent. This particular meeting place was an out-of-the-way restaurant with a small conference room where they could meet with relative privacy. They all ordered coffee, mainly to help Jason finish sobering up. Jack knew he would pay the price for having caffeine so late at night. He would not sleep well, and he would have to be careful that the caffeine didn't cause him to talk too much. This was Jason's meeting, and his depressed look at Mikey's house had changed to a look alternating between sadness and anger.

"Why?" Jason simply blurted out a single-word question.

"Why what?" Jack answered.

"Why?"

"Why what? What are you saying?"

"It seems we have a thief in our midst."

Was he talking about them? Both Jack and Bobby got nervous. You never knew with Jason how his conversations were going to end. Maybe this was one of his more paranoid times. But if he couldn't trust Jack and Bobby, who could he trust? OK, maybe they weren't entirely blameless, but this secret meeting, this version of Jason . . . it all seemed strange, and Jack thought Jason was about to lose it.

Jason's words almost seemed to drip with sadness. "Why would a person in whom you have invested your life and trust go behind your back and betray you?"

"Who did that?" Jack and Bobby almost spoke in unison. Jack thought he might know who this would be—Mikey—but he didn't know if Bobby knew, so he didn't say anything more for the moment.

Jason paused as if trying to answer his own question. Inwardly, he was asking himself: *Why me?* Why do people always take advantage of me? Why aren't I good enough?

His thoughts were interrupted.

"Jason, who are you talking about?" Bobby sounded nervous. He hoped Jason was not talking about him.

As his thoughts cleared, Jason let them know what he heard. "I went to the bathroom, and right before I closed the door, Mikey's answering machine took a message. Some dude who said he was Pete said that the shipment this week was coming in early, and what did Mikey want to do?"

"We're not scheduled for a shipment for two weeks," Jack said.

"That's right!" This was Bobby, who sounded relieved.

"Yeah. That little pervert has been stealing from us all this time." Judge and jury: that was Jason's style. He didn't really know how long this had been going on, but he just had to state his belief that it had probably been going on since Mikey joined them. It didn't matter if that was true or not. Mikey would have to pay for his greed.

Jack spoke next. "We can't let this go. What do you want to do?"

Bobby: "I think we ought to skin him alive!" Bobby was always a little dramatic. Jack didn't know if he was serious or trying to inject a little levity into the conversation. Whatever his intent, Jason's mood did not change.

"Bobby, how much do you think he's stolen?"

"Well, it depends on how long he's being doing this. Without knowing the exact amount of product he's been moving, and just going with, well . . . maybe he's been doing it for six months, I would say that it could be as much as close to a million dollars. We don't know either of those factors to be able to be exact, but that's my best guess for now."

Either the coffee was having its effect on Jason or Bobby's estimate had suddenly further sobered him up. Jason was now focused. Jack could see that he was processing the information. In serious moments, Jack thought he could see a slight twitch around Jason's left eye. He could clearly see it now. Bobby and he sat there, waiting, while Jason figured out what to do. It would not be wise to interrupt him at this moment. Jason got up from the table and began to pace. A blind man could see that his anger was rising. He balled up his fist and bit it, drawing blood, which could be seen going down his knuckles. Suddenly, he let out a yell like nothing Jack had ever heard. The next thing Jack knew, Jason was pounding a table with his bloody fist, kicking over furniture, and coming the closest to cursing that Jack had ever seen.

This went on for several minutes. One of the restaurant staff came in the room to see what this was all about. Bobby reassured him that he would take care of any damages, and escorted the guy out of the room, even as he offered weak protests to these assertions. The staff had enough experience with people like Jason that they knew their best course of action was to let his anger play out and settle the bill later.

Eventually, Jason settled down a bit, and he accepted a napkin from Jack to put on his bleeding knuckles. Jack wasn't sure if Jason had broken his hand, but he wasn't about to ask. Jason's eye twitch had subsided, which was a good thing. Now both Jack and Bobby waited for Jason to speak.

"It's obvious we cannot let this continue. You know, the hard part is that I was grooming him for a greater share of the action. If he would have been patient, he could have risen to heights he couldn't imagine." Jack wasn't sure that Jason meant all that. Jason had a way of rationalizing that always made himself look good, and one that left the object of his anger looking like a poor misguided fool.

* * * * *

Mikey liked to clean up after one of his get-togethers. He spent a good amount of time cleaning the grill, carrying trash bags, cleaning his kitchen, and generally tidying up. He never knew when he would be having another party. The next time, it could be Jason and his guys again or people from his own crew.

He noticed that he had several voice mails on his answering machine. It had been a good idea to put in a landline. If he only had his cell phone, he would have been interrupted outside when the guys were there. The one from Pete needed immediate attention, so he got on that one right away. There was a warehouse district that had fallen on hard times, and most of the buildings were empty, so there was little traffic and small chance that the deal would be discovered while it was going down. That's the building he chose to receive the shipment. Mikey would not be there, but one of his top lieutenants would do the receiving. Mikey just had to get the money together for the exchange.

The shipment was received. Meanwhile, things continued to deteriorate between Jason and Mikey. Finally, Mikey made the first move.

* * * * *

Mikey had not been untouchable. He would have gotten caught in Jack and George's earlier trap—except that he had a bona fide emergency come up that night. One of his close cousins was killed in a car accident, and Mikey had to pay his respects and comfort his aunt as best he could. It made him think about how life was far from guaranteed. Anything could happen to anyone at any time.

His involvement with Jason had been profitable for both of them. Even though he liked Jason, he felt he could do better. That's why he began to branch out on his own. His mistake was that he didn't speak to Jason before doing it. Maybe he thought Jason wouldn't approve, or maybe he just didn't think. In any case, Mikey was doing so well for himself that he didn't suspect that Jason heard the voice mail from Pete, that Jason knew all he needed to know. Even as Mikey was enjoying the material things he could obtain with his money, he was a dead man walking.

Mikey was a short fellow with tall ambitions. For one thing, he never took no for an answer. As much as that was one of his strengths, it was also his major weakness. Over time, his share of the business had grown to a place in which others in the area were complaining he was too ambitious. He was bumping into their spaces. Jason and Jack tried to reason with him until, one day, Mikey let it be known that he didn't need them or the organization. He didn't need their protection or their permission. He was ready and able to handle his own business, and he was going to do just that. If they didn't like it, Mikey said, they could go to hell.

Jason smiled when he heard this little speech. Mikey had risen fast, maybe too fast. He was so young, both in age and experience. It's always the young ones who think they know better. If you can survive the gauntlet of youthful mistakes, Jason knew, you just might have a chance of making it in the world. Too bad Mikey didn't learn from his mistakes. He didn't understand his place in the pecking order, and he really didn't understand how good he had it.

Everyone has said something that they later regretted. It wasn't long before Mikey found some of his contacts avoiding him. People who formerly admired Mikey and his tenacity became unavailable to him. His profits began to shrink. Police harassment increased, and there were days he sensed he was being followed. "Accidents" began to happen to people in his network, and product began to mysteriously disappear.

Mikey was not stupid. He suspected that Jason and Jack were behind it all. And, of course, he was right. Just as they had set him up to succeed, they set him up to fall—hard. So Mikey came back, pleading with them to let him back in, to reinstate him. He pledged allegiance and obedience. He said all the things you might hear in a B-rated mafia movie. Unfortunately for Mikey, once trust has been betrayed, it doesn't play out like it does in the movies. Jason and Jack met with him, told him they would think about it, and watched him as he left the meeting a more subdued and contrite man.

Mikey was found dead a few weeks later in his car at the bottom of the Detroit River.

Jason and Jack had never agreed on how to punish him. Word on the street was that Jason ordered a hit. No one really knew. Certainly, not Jack.

Jason met with Jack and Bobby to decide what to do about Mikey's business. After all, it had grown considerably, and now, without Mikey, they needed to put someone in place who could be trusted and bring that group in line with their plans for the entire organization. There was a long, cordial discussion. They seriously thought about handing the business over to Mikey's second-in-command, but decided against it because he had never been vetted by them. They were concerned he might have similar goals as Mikey and continue to cause trouble for them. They also talked about Jack or Bobby taking over this role. Jason vetoed that thought because, simply, they were too important to him. Eventually, they settled on George. He was the one Jack sent to film Mikey, but instead got the young teenage couple getting busted by the cops. Unknown to Jason and Jack, Bobby desperately wanted this job. This decision would come back to bite Jason and Jack.

Jack had learned a lot in what was now his two years in Detroit.

His first lesson was that he was ill-prepared for real life. He had led a sheltered life at home. His parents had tried to give him all the advantages they could, but his insistence and impatience defeated their best efforts. Every once in a while he thought about the mistakes he had made, but he never spent enough time to convince himself he was wrong in any great way.

Jack also learned he wasn't such a great judge of human character. Originally, he thought he could read people the same way a person reads a book. But he began to see that he didn't really read Jason well. Just like that, Jack was involved with people who related to Jason's values more than to the values he held. He did get one thing right: he was aware that Jason often deceived himself and lived in a world of delusion. What he didn't see was that he was more like Jason than he thought. He had long ago rejected the values he learned at home. He liked to think he was a pretty nice guy, fair and compassionate. That may have been true in the past, but if Jack were real with himself, he would admit he had transformed into a selfish and judgmental person, one full of greed and given to various temptations. For the moment, he was glad Bobby had lost his bid to take over Mikey's old territory. Maybe this was the beginning of the end of Bobby's time in the group. Once again, Jack thought he knew all the angles. But he was wrong. He was so wrong.

Jason was unaware of how he had offended Bobby. Bobby was good at playing it close to the vest. As far as Jason was concerned, things were back on track. He expected "Georgie," as some of them called him, to do a good job as new head of the southwest territory. He could increase the territory in any direction he wanted, except to the east, which belonged exclusively to Jason. Bobby would continue to make sure the numbers were correct, and Jack would continue as Jason's number two, which had always proved profitable for the both of them.

Where Jason was weak, Jack was strong. And where Jack was weak, Jason was strong. In one sense, things definitely seemed to be looking up.

NINE

Willy

"Did you hear what happened to Willy?"

It was Willy's sister, Kathy. Jack met her when he moved to Detroit, but at the time he was so wrapped up in himself that he didn't really notice her. He just knew there was talk about her taking over the family business instead of Willy. Willy was the son, and expected to step into the role, but he had frittered away his time at school, partying and chasing girls. It also became obvious that he didn't have the same skill set his father had regarding business. Willy was more artsy, like his mother. The last time they met, Jack learned that Willy had changed his major in college and was working part-time at a restaurant. His parents could afford to pay for his college, but he felt he needed to pay his way, to grow up. That's the way he put it.

"Kathy, it's been awhile. How are you doing? Are you still as smart and beautiful as I remember?"

Kathy ignored his compliment. "Jack, Willy is in the hospital." This brought Jack back to earth.

"What happened?" Jack was surprised that he was actually concerned. He and Willy had been friends, but they hadn't seen or talked to each other for a long time—more than a year—until Willy recently reached out to him. Even then, Jack could see how different they had become. Jack had a hardness to him that he didn't have when he came to Detroit, and Willy had become religious. As he thought about Willy, and his reaction to the news that his old friend was in the hospital, Kathy told him what happened.

"Willy got beat up on his way home from work two nights ago by three men."

"Was he robbed?" That had to be the only reason anyone would mug Willy. If you knew him, he was always a nice guy.

"No. We thought that was it, but they didn't take his money. It was worse."

"So why did they beat him? Did he offend them some way, and they were getting even?"

"You could say that. They beat him so bad that they broke a rib. They punched him with brass knuckles or something, kicked him, and left him all bruised and bloody."

Jack couldn't believe what he was hearing. Why would anybody do that to Willy? Was he living a double life or something?

Kathy was usually pretty steady emotionally, but now her voice broke and she could hardly contain herself.

"They hit him with a bat and cracked his skull. Jack, there is swelling of the brain, and we don't know if he is going to survive." She was crying by now.

Jack's mind and emotions were swirling. He still didn't know why anyone would do this to Willy, and his emotions were ranging from feelings of revenge and anger to extreme sadness. Sometimes, it felt like everything was happening at the same time. As his eyes swelled with tears, Jack was glad he was on the phone and Kathy could not see him. He was also thinking of how he was going to get some of his guys together and find the people who did this. He had to be strong for Kathy. Composing himself, he asked Kathy where Willy was.

"He's in ICU at the Detroit Medical Center. Mom and Dad are there, and I'm going there this afternoon."

Jack could go there right away, but he decided against it. He needed to get his thoughts together and develop a plan. He would have to talk with Jason and see who he would recommend that Jack bring together to find the people that did this to Willy. Jack had never killed anyone. He wanted to do all he could short of that. He didn't know if Michigan had capital punishment. If it did, he couldn't think of anyone worth dying for, which would be exactly what would happen to him if he was ever convicted of murder.

"Jack, could you stop by to see him? He is in an induced coma right now, and they are waiting to see if the brain swelling goes down, but I think he would sense your presence, and it would help. Mom and Dad would enjoying seeing you again, too, not to mention me."

Jack had never visited someone in the hospital. Even the guys who got injured at work didn't get a visit from him. Once he thought of sending a card, but that seemed corny.

"Kathy, I will be there, but not today. I promise. I'll be there tomorrow. I have to wrap up some things before then. I hope you understand."

Kathy had settled down some, and she said that would be fine. Maybe Willy would be out of his coma by then. She said she would let her parents know, and she would work her schedule so she could be there too.

"Thank you, Jack. See you tomorrow."

Jason was vaguely moved by Jack's story. You could tell he cared, but he didn't care that much. His only concern was how such a get-even move would impact the business. After all, since Mikey died, Jason was only interested in making sure there were no other troublemakers in the ranks.

"Jack, if there were three guys who jumped your friend, I would say take maybe five guys with you in case you run into them at the same time. Don't take any guns, you don't want someone to get crazy. But I would make sure you had knives, brass knuckles, that kind of thing. I'll talk around the place and see if we can get you some guys that know how to handle themselves and keep their mouths shut." They both agreed that Jack would find the people who beat up Willy and come up with a plan.

* * * * *

Jack was not able to get to the hospital until late afternoon the next day. It had been a hectic day. He had to make sure George knew what he was doing and how to start with his new group. Jack knew it was important for a new leader to come in and establish his authority early. There were sure to be guys in the group who thought they were better suited for replacing Mikey. Some had not met George before, so that made it all the more challenging. George would have to be both diplomatic and tough in his approach. It would be a hard dance.

When Jack got to the Detroit Medical Center, Willy was still in a coma and in ICU. His parents had spent the night. The hospital provided cots for them to sleep on, but you could tell they hadn't slept much. Kathy was also there. She had come immediately after work. She was glad to see Jack. He wasn't sure her parents were glad to see him, but they didn't give any indication they weren't. In fact, it seemed quite the opposite. Even as they looked tired, they seemed relieved Jack was there. He wasn't sure what all that meant. Kathy spoke first.

"Jack, we are so glad to see you. We found out that they only allow two people at a time to go in and see William." In front of her parents, she always referred to Will as William. They said that if they wanted to name him Will, they would have. William was the name they gave him, and that's the name they expected him to go by.

"Mr. and Mrs. James, I am so sorry that this happened. I wanted to be here sooner, but I couldn't get away until now." Jack wanted to say the right things and be supportive, but his words had a hollow ring. When he left their house, there had been tension between him and Will's mom. And he hadn't kept in touch with them. Once they invited him over for Thanksgiving, but he didn't think they really meant it, so he didn't go. He didn't even RSVP. As far as anyone knew, he had fallen off the face of the earth. Now was not a good time to pretend that everything was fine between them. He would not be surprised if they told him to leave.

But that isn't what happened. Both of Will's parents were quite welcoming. They both hugged him, and he could see that Mrs. James had been crying and was about to start again. She reached in her purse for the overused tissues she kept there.

"Jack, we have thought so much about you," she said. "So many things have happened since you left. When this is over, we will have to have you over for dinner and catch up. God has been so good."

"Yes, ma'am. That would be good." Jack could not believe what he was hearing. *Someone had thought of him?* He had hardened his heart to the point that all he knew was that no one cared about him anymore. Even his parents, by now, had surely disowned him. He was so bad at keeping in touch that he believed they had written him off. Now, here he was in a hospital, and he had an invitation to dinner with the last decent people that he had let down. But what took him most by surprise was Mrs. James's statement, "God has been so good." Her only son was in a coma in ICU, his chances of survival slim, and God was good? What a crutch! *Oh well,* Jack thought. *People deal with tragedy in their own way. To each his own.*

He wasn't sure if they could tell that he was wrestling with so many thoughts, and he was doing his best to present a calm, controlled front. He thought it would be better to turn his attention to Kathy.

"Has there been any change?"

"It's been up and down. Different doctors have been in to see him. Once or twice I saw the nurses working on him like something had gone wrong. They are saying little, even when I ask specific questions. I guess no news is good news."

"That's not good enough!" Jack blurted out. "They should at least answer your questions. I'm going to find someone and find out what's going on." Jack had seen this before. Sick people dealing with doctors who apparently slept through their class on bedside manners. He didn't realize that he was still angry about the way his family was treated when his younger brother broke his leg. As far as they knew, Don could have lost his leg, and the doctors wouldn't tell them anything. Maybe those doctors graduated at the bottom of their class, and their behavior was the exception, but the result was that Jack had little confidence in the medical system. He was going to become a pain until he found out something he could tell the family.

The next time one of the doctors came by, Jack cornered him and asked about Will. The doctor asked if he was family, and it was all Jack could do to keep from physically attacking the man. Of course, the doctor didn't know this because Jack had learned how to keep his composure in difficult situations. When you are running the streets with unsavory characters, you learn quickly which facade to use in the various situations you encounter. Jack was with Kathy at the time, so he referred the doctor to her, and they both learned that the swelling had gone down some, but the doctors weren't sure if there was residual damage. They were keeping Will in a coma for a few more days. When the swelling went down some more, they would begin to slowly bring him out of the coma and test his cognition, reflexes, and much more. This was better news, for they now could plan. The Jameses wanted someone from the family to be there at all times in case something happened. Because Jack was there, they incorporated him in the rotation.

Kathy's parents left to get something to eat, and that left Jack alone with her. He took the opportunity to press her again for some answers.

"Kathy, you never really answered my question the other day."

"What was that?"

"Why did he get beat up by those people? You told me they didn't take his money, that he was on his way home from work. You gave me details about his injuries, but you never answered why he had been attacked."

"I'm so sorry. I had so many thoughts swirling through my head. It took me a while to find your contact information, I needed to sort things out at home so my parents could be at the hospital, I had to settle some things at work. I really didn't mean to ignore you."

"So?"

"So what?"

"So why did he get attacked? Do you even know the answer?"

"Oh yes. I know the answer. They beat him up because he is a Christian."

* * * * *

While Jack was trying to wrap his head around what Kathy had just told him, in a different place in another area of Detroit, a new Christian was trying to be faithful. Margaret knew Jack, but not well. She did not know that Jack was keeping Jason's secrets. He had done so well. When Margaret became a Christian, she made it her mission to share her faith with anyone she knew, including Jack. This was especially important to her because, even though Jason liked some of the changes in her life since she converted, he was not willing to follow her. He believed she would get over this change sooner or later. But it was starting to look like, if this happened at all, it would be much later. Margaret figured that maybe Jack would be more receptive. If he decided to follow Jesus, it couldn't help but influence Jason.

As part of her plan, she introduced Miriam to Jack. Maybe between the two of them, Jack would come to Christ sooner. The three of them didn't get together much, but when they did, the gospel always came up in conversations—one way or the other. Miriam and Margaret talked so much about it that Jack often decided to quit hanging out with them. Besides, Margaret was living with his business partner.

But something else was going on: although he didn't acknowledge it, Jack kept finding himself attracted to the message. Another good thing was that whenever Jack did see Margaret, it was never just him and her. Miriam was always there.

Jack did give thought to what they shared. He had good arguments, but so did they. What bothered him was that they not only had decent arguments of their own, their lives showed a change—a peace—that he only wished he could have.

Jack eventually decided that most of what they said could easily be explained by the fact that they were women. Women were more emotional than men. Religion—apart from the leadership—was mostly peopled by women, so it was only logical that Margaret and Miriam be attracted to it. He didn't know Miriam as well, but he knew Margaret came from an insecure background, and a figure like Jesus would be attractive to her. Jesus was a crutch, and Jack didn't need a crutch. He could stand on his own.

He had more of a struggle explaining Will's family. That whole family had "gotten saved." Maybe he could argue that Will was weak, but his Dad was a man's man. His construction business prospered because of his hard work. You couldn't succeed in that business without being strong, both physically and mentally. Jack told himself he would have to think more about that. Sooner or later, he would figure it out, and all the pieces of the puzzle would fall in place for him. Then he could talk intelligently with Will and his family and convince them that although they were well intentioned, they were wrong.

Meanwhile, Jack was taking his turn sitting at the hospital with Will. Kathy—and the doctors agreed with her on this—was certain that having someone who Will knew stay with him most of the time would be helpful. Studies showed that, even in a coma, people recognize voices. Jack would talk with Will's parents when they were there, or Kathy when she came. He really liked talking with Kathy. She was quite intelligent, and pretty, but he tried not to focus that much on the latter. When he was by himself, he spoke more directly to Will, hoping that maybe he would wake up when he was there. He told him what he was doing, but he wouldn't mention his life of crime. He had to be careful to pull that off. He would ask philosophical questions, as if Will could answer back. Eventually, Jack would look at Will, with all the tubes in him, the medical equipment beeping and buzzing in the background, and wonder what was the meaning of it all. He didn't speak much about religion. He was tired of that topic.

****

Jack found himself spending more time with Kathy, partly by default since they were at the hospital together much of the time. He found himself more and more attracted to her. After a while, he wished he had gotten to know her sooner instead of ignoring her when they lived under the same roof. To be truthful, she was younger than his sister, and it didn't seem right that he should chase after her when her family had been gracious enough to let him live with them for a time.

Kathy had growing feelings for Jack, too. She had to be careful, though. In the short time since she became a follower of Christ, she had learned that her heart could deceive her. She needed to guard against that, to not be led by her feelings. Also, in a home Bible study she attended, there was mention of not being "unequally yoked." She learned it meant that she shouldn't be dating someone who didn't share her faith or values. She didn't really know Jack well or his views on Christ. She was of the opinion that Jack was like a lot of guys she knew, pretty much wrapped up in themselves, always trying to prove how manly they were. Maybe it was a phase. She hoped so.

Their discussions usually revolved around Will. They looked for any evidence that he recognized them, that he might be coming out of his coma. Sometimes his eyes opened slightly, and they thought he was looking at them. After a while, they concluded it was probably nothing.

Kathy would sometimes pray out loud. The first time Jack heard her, he thought she was talking to him. Then he thought she was talking to Will. When he realized she was praying, it partly shocked—and intrigued—him. This shocked him because he had never heard anyone pray out loud, except for grace over the meal at Thanksgiving. (And those were usually short and quick, empty words, really, as far as he was concerned.) But Kathy's prayer intrigued him because she seemed sincere, and she spoke as if she was talking to someone. Kathy didn't change her normal tone of voice or use big words or do any of those things that Jack imagined were required if and when you prayed. When he asked her about it, she told him that talking to God was like talking to your best friend. She told him quite a bit about praying, but one thing really stuck with him. She said that you could tell God anything, and He wouldn't hold it against you. Jack wished he had a friend like that. He spent most days walking on eggshells in his relationships. He couldn't tell anyone some of the things he was thinking or doing.

Once in a while, Kathy's father was there alone with Jack. Jack felt both more comfortable with him and challenged by him. It wasn't so much what he said. Like most men, he tended to be direct in his communications, and he didn't spend a lot of time talking about every aspect of a subject. He viewed life as a series of problems that needed fixing. (This got him in trouble at home sometimes. His wife and daughter might bring up a subject, and he would think they were presenting a problem that needed fixing, and he would be the designated fixer. More often than not, they just wanted him to hear them, and maybe say some words of encouragement. It was a running joke in their family how he consistently misread such situations.)

He did not have that struggle with William or Jack. He could be himself and not second-guess what had been said or expected. From Jack's perspective, this man was the total package. He was smart and creative. He was successful in business. He could focus on a problem and push aside distractions. He had a good family. He was even married to the same woman longer than anyone Jack knew except for his own parents. He admired him, and hoped that maybe, someday, he could be like him. Maybe not in all things, though. Jack was surprised the first time he was alone with Mr. James in the ICU. They were with Will, and Mr. James laid his hand on Will's head and began to pray out loud. *What is it with these people?* Jack thought to himself. He had never seen someone put hands on another person and pray for them. He didn't want to seem ignorant, so he decided not to ask him about it, but instead wait until he could talk to Kathy. Jack found this happening: his concept of being a man was being challenged.

Kathy got busy at work and couldn't come to the hospital for another two days. They had to redo the visitation schedule so Jack spent the next day with Will by himself. He was pleasantly surprised when Mrs. James came by with a home-cooked meal for him. Jack knew how to cook, but only barely. Just enough to keep from starving. Mostly, he ate at restaurants. Even her home-cooked meal was a wonderful thing indeed. Mrs. James couldn't stay long, she said, because she was on the way to meet her husband at a group prayer meeting. Again, just when Jack thought he understood some things, he realized there was a lot he did not know.

Despite all this, Jack thought he had his life pretty much under control. He was making lots of money working with Jason, and he was enjoying the perks of his prosperity. He had a nice car, could date just about any girl he wanted, and guys in the organization respected and feared him. He liked that he could have just about anything he wanted. Yes, sir, the plans he had when he left home were now pretty much coming to pass. He was somebody, and the sky was the limit.

But little did Jack know that all the material things and relationships were much shallower than he thought. He actually made himself believe that people liked him for things other than the power he wielded or the money he could send their way. The women in his life were not the types of girls his mother would approve of, and his relationship with Jason was not as solid as he thought.

But the most dangerous threat to Jack was not his blind side of misinterpreting the affections of the people around him. The most dangerous threat was not even that Bobby had plans to push him aside.

The most dangerous threat was that he had hardened his conscience. There had been a time he believed in right and wrong, and he had easily recognized those things. There was a time he felt convicted about the wrongness of some of the things he did, but that time was now long past. The conviction and guilt now seemed like mists that quickly disappeared. He had no qualms about stepping on people as he made his way up in the world. He decided he needed to watch out for Number One, and that number one was himself. In the beginning, Jack believed he could work with people, build a consensus, and everyone would be lifted up equally. This was no longer his belief. Now he watched out for himself, and if anyone else benefited from his actions, it was purely coincidental.

So, as Jack increased his bank account and enjoyed some of the finer things in life, the end of the road was fast approaching. He was soon to see how fragile his "kingdom" had become.

* * * * *

Bobby continued in his central role in the organization, but he disliked that Jack looked on him as third in the group. Both of them knew that part of his role was to double-check Jack's numbers, and Jack didn't seem to mind this. Two sets of eyes couldn't hurt—or so he thought. What he didn't know was that Bobby was cooking the numbers in such a way that it looked like Jack was skimming more of the profit for himself than was agreed. Jason thought he was getting the lion's share of the take, and he was, but Bobby's numbers made it look like Jack was. It didn't help Jack that he was experimenting with his own crew. Nothing big, but enough to cast suspicion on his motives.

Bobby learned a lot about Jason through the Mikey episode. Jason had never expressed himself in front of Bobby like he did when he overheard the phone message on Mikey's phone. Bobby thought Jason was fairly rational and considered all the facts in a calm, controlled manner before making business decisions. Jason was not that way at all. His decisions were primarily emotion-driven. When he felt like moving in a certain direction, he would ask Jack and Bobby what they thought, but facts and understanding were not the overriding factors.

How Jason felt drove the train. This was both a strength and a weakness. Jason liked to say that he went by his gut. He took big gambles, and what kept him afloat was that more of them succeeded than failed. An outsider might look at his decision-making processes and come to the conclusion that his decisions were just barely informed guesses—and that person would be right.

This impulsiveness of Jason's would serve Bobby well. So would Jason's paranoia and distrust of others. Since childhood, those he trusted had left him. Starting with his father and mother, Jason experienced a long list of people who let him down at some critical juncture of his life. Most people would forgive in many of those situations, but Jason had never seen forgiveness modeled, so he defaulted to distrusting people and using them as he felt he had been used by others. His distrust of others grew into paranoia. Not only were people untrustworthy, they were also out to get him. That's why Jason could never have friends for long. That's why he kept Margaret at a distance. All this time, and she still believed that he worked odd hours in a warehouse. It was somewhat of a miracle that his relationship with Jack lasted as long as it did. Jack may have thought that their friendship was deeper than it was. Jason viewed authentic friendship as him using someone else for his benefit. Most likely, Jason's friendship with Jack was based on Jack's good instincts and people skills. Jack would be wrong in thinking it was more than that.

* * * * *

"He's awake!" Kathy nearly shouted into the phone.

"Really? When?"

"Just a while ago. I called you as soon as the doctors came in. They're working on him now. Can you come soon?"

Jack looked at the time. He still had some numbers to crunch to get them over to Bobby, and a couple of places to visit for an upcoming delivery later in the week.

"Kathy, I'll be there as soon as I can. Are your parents there?"

"They're on the way. They've only had a little sleep, but I had to call them and tell them. They insisted to be told immediately if anything changed. This is the change we've all been waiting for!"

Kathy was as excited and happy about Will waking up as she had been sad and distraught about him getting beaten up. A small smile crossed Jack's lips. She was an interesting girl indeed.

"OK, I better go so I can finish up a few things around here and get there soon."

"Hurry!"

Will and Kathy's parents got there just a few minutes after she hung up with Jack. She told them that Jack was on the way, and that the doctors were in with William.

"What happened when William woke up? Did he say anything to you?" Will's mom asked.

"He just let out a groan and opened his eyes. I said his name, and he looked at me and said my name. Then he groaned again and closed his eyes."

They asked her a million questions, but they were asking the wrong person. That was all she could tell them. She had been sitting with Will for several hours and had been on the verge of falling asleep in the chair when it all happened. Now she was as excited as they were, but as for any more information, she was an empty vessel.

They sat in the ICU waiting room with other people there for friends and loved ones. Every once in a while a medical person would come out and everyone would perk up, some fearful, some expectantly, but all hoping to hear good news about their loved one's progress. Kathy and her parents were no different. Most of the people knew them as being the people with the son in a coma who had been there the longest. Both Kathy and her parents hoped they were being a good witness for Christ to the people who joined them in the room. They weren't ashamed of being followers of Christ. They also didn't want to bring shame to Christ. They had heard the admonition, "You may be the only Bible some people ever read."

Finally, they saw one of the doctors who had been attending Will. They strained to see what his body language said as he came toward them.

"The good news is that he is awake," the doctor said. "It was good that Kathy was there when it happened so we could give him immediate attention." That really wasn't much more than what Kathy had told them! They were looking for any crumbs of progress.

"What else? Can we go in and see him? Is he going to be all right?" Mrs. James was trying to be strong, but her voice was cracking. Mr. James was staring a hole through the doctor.

"It's too early to tell. We will have to run tests to see, to what extent, if any, he suffered brain damage." They did not want to hear this. What they wanted to hear was that Will had woken from the coma and asked for his mother and father, that he asked for chicken noodle soup, that he asked to get up and get a snack. That's what they wanted to hear. That he was as normal as he was before he got beat up.

"Can we see him?"

"Yes, but don't expect much. He is pretty sedated, and coming completely out of a coma can take some time." Mr. James was still staring a hole through the doctor.

When Jack showed up, they all spent a good amount of time with Will. Mrs. James was visibly distressed, though she tried to hide it. Mr. James was acting the strong, silent one. He knew his wife, and he had to maintain his composure for her sake. He would have to deal with his emotions later. He and Jack spoke briefly.

Jack was watching their reaction. He didn't know if he would hold up as well as they were. In a way, he was reading them. He wondered how much of their strength they were getting from their faith. He wasn't much for religious stuff. But he was allowing himself to think more about it.

He enjoyed the time he spent with Kathy. When she wasn't fretting about Will, she was fun to be with. Their relationship had grown, and even though Kathy wasn't sure what Jack did for a living or his stance on Christ, she thought there might be a possibility of going deeper in their relationship. And then . . . she would come back to reality. What Jack did for a living could be negotiable. But his stance on Christ would be a deal-breaker. She had a strong feeling that Jack was not like her and her family in this regard.

Will was improving slowly. Sometimes it was two steps forward and one step back. There were people and churches praying for his recovery, but Jack didn't know anything about that except a little bit about the prayer meeting that Mrs. James said she and Will's dad attended. He really didn't know what they did except maybe pray. He asked Kathy about it, and it confirmed her suspicions of his view of Christianity. If Jack didn't know that people prayed at a prayer meeting, he surely didn't know anything about the object of their prayers. It was funny, but it was not, she thought. It looked like there was no future with him unless Jack could somehow change—or she was willing to compromise her faith.

During one of the quiet times that they sat with Will, Kathy stood and asked Jack to stand with her next to Will's bedside. Jack did not know what was about to happen, and Kathy took little time to explain.

"Here, take my hand." She took his hand more than Jack taking hers. He noticed that her hand was soft; it had a nurturing feel to it. Before he knew what was happening, she took her other hand and placed it on Will's forehead.

"Father God," she said, "Will is your son. He is here in this bed because he is a follower of Jesus. He wasn't looking for a fight. The doctors say they don't know if or how he will come out of this. We choose to trust you and believe your Word. You said that wherever two are together in your name that you would be there, and that if we ask anything in your name, you would do it. Well, we're here, and we're asking. And we are standing against the enemy, and we are fully expecting a complete recovery for Will. Glorify yourself in his body. By your wounds we are healed, and we claim that for him right now, in Jesus' name."

Jack even found himself mumbling, "Amen."

Jack was surprised at what had just happened, but it was nothing compared to what happened next. He had a mouthful of questions to send Kathy's way about what just took place. But before he could start speaking, he heard a voice.

"Kathy! Jack! Hey, so glad to see you. What happened? What am I doing here?" Will had just noticed that he was in a hospital bed, and he had enough tubes in him that he knew something serious had happened.

Jack sat down. Or maybe he really fell down and the chair caught him. Kathy was crying and praising God and jumping up and down. Will was still talking.

"I have a lot to tell you. I've been places. I've seen things. I even saw dead people."

Jack was glad he was sitting down. He had gone from surprised to stunned.

About that time, an ICU nurse came in because she heard the commotion from Kathy. She wondered if Will had gone into a seizure and knocked over some of the monitoring equipment. When she learned what actually happened, she put on her professional face and told Kathy she would have to compose herself. She didn't have to say anything to Jack. He was just staring at Will, who was busy trying to remove tubes from his body. The nurse didn't like that—at all. She told him to lie down, she would call the doctor, and they would address his needs. There was a moment, though, when Jack thought he glimpsed a tear in the nurse's eye. He wondered what he was going to tell Jason and his friends. *Nobody will ever believe me*, he thought.

The rest was a blur. Kathy called her parents to tell them what happened, but Jack could tell they were not getting it. She kept repeating herself and saying, "Yes, Yes! It's true. . . . No! No! He is all right! He really is! God did it!" Every few minutes, she would say, "Thank you, Jesus!" Meanwhile, several doctors and medical personnel came into the room and began to work on Will, which included many questions about how he was doing, how he felt, and more. Slowly, they began to take out some tubes, one by one. Jack got a little nauseous when they removed Will's breathing tube.

"Are you all right, sir?" the nurse asked.

She had to repeat the question. Jack had somehow spaced out.

"Sir, you will have to leave the room. We have to do some things, and we need the room."

"Yes, ma'am." Jack got up from his chair and heard the nurse say the same thing to Kathy. They went back to the waiting room, with Kathy still saying, "Praise you, Jesus!" and Jack trying to figure out how what just happened had happened.

The Jameses arrived sooner than Kathy and Jack expected. Kathy and Jack would find out later they had ignored the speed limits. When they got there, they were both crying. Kathy joined in with the tears, and they had a group hug. Jack didn't know if the wetness on his shirt was their tears—or if he had cried a bit as well.

TEN

Bobby Makes His Move

It is said that one should not let a good crisis go to waste. Mikey's death and Will's accident gave Bobby room to maneuver closer to Jason at Jack's expense. Bobby took advantage of Jack's frequent absences to undermine him. He had Jason's ear more often, and Jason was trusting him more and more. There were a few decisions where Jack was not available to give input. Bobby's counsel turned out to be just the thing Jason needed—and wanted—to hear.

"Boss, I got some bad news." On one particular meeting, Bobby decided he would make his move. Jack was spending a lot of time at the hospital, taking his turn waiting for Will to come out of his coma. Bobby took advantage, telling Jason pieces of negative things about Jack. It was like a farmer planting a crop. He knew that if he planted the right seed and watered and weeded it, he would reap the crop he wanted. Someone once told him that if he wanted corn, he needed to plant corn. He would not get corn by planting tomatoes. It was kind of corny, but he got the point. He would plant information about Jack in Jason's ear so Jason would not be able to come to any conclusion other than that Jack was betraying him. Over time, Bobby had been slowly doing that. Now was the time to tell him what he hoped would push him over the line from suspicion to certainty.

"I've been checking the numbers since before Mikey, and it seems like Jack knew all along what Mikey was doing."

"What do you mean?"

"Well, look at these. Every time Mikey made money, Jack's account would increase too."

"So what are you saying? That Jack was getting a cut of Mikey's profits?"

"That's exactly what it looks like. But that's not all. Jack wasn't ever around between the scheduled product drops. By itself, it doesn't look like much, but with the bump in his account, I wonder if he was helping Mikey receive shipments that were unknown to you or me."

Bobby could tell Jason was processing the information his usual way, and that it was having the desired effect. Jason's eye began to twitch, and he had that faraway look he got when he was becoming convinced that, once again, someone had betrayed him.

"This can't be true. Is it?"

"There's no other way to look at it. Isn't it convenient that his old friend ended up in the hospital? Do you really think he has to be gone as much as he is? And by the way, neither of us has been to the hospital to see if it's even true, or if he's been there as often as he says. He may even be planning with Georgie to take over. Remember, it was Jack who recommended that Georgie take over Mikey's crew."

Bobby didn't have anything on George, but if he could take him down as well, it would be an added bonus.

Up to that point, there was a chance that Jason would reject Bobby's concerns, but when he threw in George's name, in Jason's mind it became a conspiracy. He could not let that go. His whole empire was at risk. His close confidant and the number two man in the organization was plotting to take over. Jason could not stomach the thought. After all they had been through, all the close calls with the police and other dealers, now this! He would deal with George later, but first he had to teach Jack that no matter how high you go in the organization, Jason could take it all away.

"What do you want to do?" Bobby had to make sure Jason owned the decision of what to do next. If he was lucky, Bobby was thinking, he would be able to remove Jason as well and establish himself as the head of all that the three of them had worked hard to achieve. *Just give him enough rope*, Bobby thought . . .

Jason left their discussion depressed and angry. On one of the few times that Margaret could remember, he came home and moped around the apartment. Something was going on, and she didn't know what it was. Maybe he had been passed over for a promotion at work. Or worse, he could have been fired. She thought about what she might say if he opened up to her about it. The poor girl: she still didn't know Jason hadn't worked at the warehouse for more than a year.

She had given up on telling him about Christ. Every time she brought it up, he would retreat into himself or become angry at her. It was obvious the subject made him uncomfortable. She limited herself to praying for him and serving him. Miriam had told her that she might win him by her godly behavior, but she didn't see any movement in that direction either. If anything, Jason had more frequent and even louder outbursts. Today, she didn't know what to expect.

Miriam came over later in the day. They had decided it was the best time of the day to get together for a Bible study. Margaret would have called and cancelled, but she forgot to write it down, so when Miriam knocked on the door, she was as surprised as Jason.

Jason did not like Miriam. He didn't know her well, and rarely saw her, but he felt she was the one responsible for putting crazy ideas about religion into Margaret's head. For a while, when Margaret dared speak to him about religion, he was sure he was hearing Miriam. *Oh great! Another problem to deal with!* he reasoned to himself.

So, within minutes of Miriam arriving, Jason made up some excuse about having to get something at work, and left the apartment.

* * * * *

"Jack, call me when you get this message. We need to talk." Jack missed the call from Jason when he was at the hospital. He figured it must have come in when all the excitement was going on. It could have been when he stopped at the watering hole near his apartment. He looked at his watch. It was past 10 PM. It was late to call, but Jason didn't like to be kept waiting. As it was, Jack was sure to hear something from him about why he didn't call earlier.

"Yeah, Jason, I just got your voice mail."

"Man, it's past ten o'clock. Why didn't you call earlier?"

"The message just came in." Jack lied, but he was in no mood to hear Jason ramble on about his needing to get back to him sooner. Jason liked to paint a picture of himself as being super important, and by extension, his phone calls were super important. Jack didn't want to play that game today. Besides, he was still trying to figure out how Will came out of his coma, and was suddenly nearly normal, as though nothing had happened. *What did he mean that he had been places, seen things, and seen dead people?* Jack would get his chance to learn what really happened when things settled down at the hospital.

"Can you get over to the warehouse on Fifth Street?" This was one of the places they liked to use when they needed to meet about something important. Jack couldn't figure out what was so important that they had to meet on the other side of the city. He was tired. He wanted to go to sleep. He was hoping this could wait until tomorrow. Jack had stopped at a bar on the way home from the hospital. In his inebriated state, he tried to put it off until morning.

"Well, I can tell that you've been drinking, and I know I've been drinking. It seems to me we would be better off by waiting until tomorrow when our heads are a little clearer."

They talked about it a bit more, and Jack finally gave in.

"OK, but it's going to take a bit for me to get there. I need to take a shower and clean up a bit. I can be there in about an hour." Jack wondered who "we" were—Jason had said something about "we" in the call . . . who exactly was going to be there. Georgie was doing fairly well of late. He hoped that George hadn't done anything to get himself in trouble. Neither Jason nor Jack liked having to clean up the messes made by others.

And so, Jack eventually made his way to the warehouse, was confronted by Jason, the call came in from Margaret, infuriating Jason all the more, Jack's face was smashed by the first punch, and then he was dragged into the alley. The beating began . . .

* * * * *

When Jack woke up, he could hear, but couldn't see, and the only reason he didn't think he was paralyzed was the intense pain he felt all over his body. The pain also convinced him that he wasn't dead—yet. No matter. He would welcome dying to be rid of this kind of pain.

He couldn't remember what happened. He didn't recognize the voices he heard. They sounded focused and professional. He wished he could think clearer. There were moments of sharp pain, as if he was being moved. He wished he could see. At first, he thought he was blind, but now he was beginning to realize his eyes were swollen shut, and they had something on them. *Could those be bandages?* Then he heard it; a siren. Was he moving? Was he in an ambulance? The pain was subsiding. Was he dying? *Is this how it feels to die?* Jack was indeed in an ambulance. And though he had no way to know it, he was on the way to the same hospital and ICU that Will was in. The pain medicine was doing its job, and Jack fell asleep.

* * * * *

Jack woke up in the ICU, but he didn't know it at first. His face was still bandaged, and he was groggy from all the pain medicine they were giving him. After a while, he thought he felt other things attached to his body, but he couldn't really tell what they were. It was silent around him, except for the sounds of machines, but he didn't know if those were near or far. Once in a while he thought he heard someone crying in the distance. It was all extremely disorienting, but gradually he began to remember some of what had happened. He thought he must have been in a car accident on the way to the hospital to see Will, but then he remembered that Will had experienced a sudden healing, and that there had been a lot of excitement. He was working on trying to figure out what happened when he heard someone calling his name. It was the ICU nurse asking if he was awake. Jack tried to answer. That's when he realized he couldn't move his mouth. He also felt pain when he tried to move his lips. All that came out was some mixture of grunt and moan. It sure would have been nice to know ahead of time that he couldn't speak. Nevertheless, that was enough for the nurse to know that he was no longer unconscious. She began to talk to him.

"Mr. Olsen, we're glad you are back with the living." *Is she kidding?*

Had he died and come back? Jack was glad for the pain medicine, but he wished he could think more clearly.

"The doctor will be here shortly to tell you all you want to know. I can tell you that you're lucky to be alive. The paramedics lost you a few times on the way here. I can also tell you that you are in one of the best hospitals in the country, and that you will receive the best care." She did not tell Jack much more than that. He was still struggling to figure out how he got so hurt. Since he couldn't see with all the bandages on his face, and couldn't talk, he was basically stuck waiting and trying to figure things out for himself. He wondered when they would give him more pain medicine.

* * * * *

There had been a lot of excitement around Will's healing. Instead of staying in the hospital for a long time, he was released with a full bill of health less than a week after he came out of his coma. He would have chosen to be released earlier, but they kept wanting to run tests on him because they couldn't believe he was well. Kathy wanted to share the adventure with Jack, but it was like he had disappeared into thin air the day of Will's healing. The Jameses were also perplexed at Jack's disappearance. They wondered if it was something they had said or done, or if Jack was so insensitive as to take off without letting them know.

Meanwhile, in Jack's world, he wasn't even sure what hospital he was in.

It was a few days, and several bandage changes, before Jack could see some light through his eyelids. They had swollen shut so tightly that just trying to pull them open was useless. He was now able to talk well enough to be understood most of the time. It was still painful, and he was frustrated that his body was so broken, but at least he could sense that, somehow, he was getting better. His pain was still being controlled with medication. He heard the nurses talking once and saying they were concerned he might get addicted to the meds.

A lady from the admissions office came to see Jack when he was able to communicate. She asked him all the normal stuff: next of kin, emergency contact, allergies, and much more. Jack refused to give her his parents' information; he did not want them to see him this way. Besides, it would be more than awkward if the first thing they heard of him was that he was in the hospital and he couldn't even tell them what happened to get him in that spot. Jack still could not remember much anyway, so he was not able to tell the admissions woman much.

Meanwhile, he was trying to get something clearer in his mind. *Wiley... Wheeley... Willing? Willing to... what?* His mind was playing tricks with him, maybe? *Winston? Wilson? Williamson?* He was trying to remember. *William?... Will?...* Jack fell asleep.

*****

His doctor kept him in ICU because of his amnesia until they finally decided to move him into a room where he could still be monitored but his care not prove so costly to the hospital. And day by day, Jack's physical wounds continued to heal.

And then he realized they were standing in front of him. At least he *thought* there were two of them. His sight was sometimes blurry, at best, and many times he saw double. Who were these two women? They weren't dressed like hospital staff. As he tried to focus his sight, he noticed that there weren't two women, but one, and she was attractive. He stared at her. Kathy would later say that it seemed like he was looking through her instead of at her. He didn't say anything, but he used all his mental energy trying to figure who this person was.

"Jack?"

She knew his name. *Who is she?*

"Jack, can you hear me? It's me, Kathy."

Unexpectedly, he felt tears forming in his eyes. "I'm . . . sorry. I don't know who you are."

Kathy tried to retain her composure. "I'm Kathy James. Will's sister."

"Will." *There's that name again.* Jack's mind began racing. He felt he knew that name, but he couldn't remember from where. Jack was so frustrated that he almost asked this Kathy to leave. She continued speaking before he had a chance to do so.

"I'm sorry you don't remember me, but I know who you are. You're Jack Olsen, and you know my brother Will. It's because of him that you came to Detroit. You and Will went your separate ways for about a year, and then Will contacted you to let you know that he had become a Christian, as the rest of our family did. You weren't all that impressed." She smiled. "Then Will got beat up real bad by some thugs because he was a follower of Christ. He ended up in ICU at this same hospital, and you came and visited him for a long time. Then he got miraculously healed. You were there when it happened. That's the last I saw you—until today."

Bits of the story made sense to Jack. He very well could know this Will. Why else would his name have been on his mind? He vaguely remembered talking to some girls about religion—but this girl wasn't one of them.

Jack was able to croak out a few questions. "I visited Will in ICU for a long time? Were your parents there?" He asked about her parents because he was beginning to remember an older couple, and he assumed they were her parents.

"Yes, we took turns so somebody was always with Will, since he was in a coma, and we wanted someone to be there when he came out of it."

Jack was starting to put the pieces together. "Where is Will?"

"He's at work. He said that if I found that you were really *you*, that I was to call and let him know. You don't know how hard we've been trying to find you."

Jack finally knew somebody who knew him! What he still didn't know was how he got hurt—or how they had been able to find him.

"Kathy, I'm sorry. I'm tired. I need to sleep. You've been like an angel, but I'm going to have to ask you to come back later. My head hurts from all the stuff you've told me today. Let me think on it, and we can pick up again the next time you visit, if you're willing."

If I'm willing? Kathy thought to herself. She wanted to grab him and hug him and kiss him all at once, but she didn't want to reveal her true feelings for him since he had never indicated as much interest in her, and there was still the problem of his lack of a relationship with Christ. Not to mention that, for the most part, he still didn't remember her. He was going on what she was telling him. If there was ever going to be anything between them, they would have to start from scratch.

"I'm sorry I tired you out," Kathy said. "I'll be back tomorrow. I'll let Will and the folks know we found you." She touched his arm and said goodbye. His sight was very focused as he watched her leave.

When she was gone, Jack's mind started whirling. So he *did* know somebody in Detroit. It sounded like he knew a whole family, aside from his own. Even in his amnesia, he remembered that he had a brother and sister, a mother and father. He wondered why he didn't want them contacted; the nurses told him this had been his request. He figured Will must have been a good friend. Why else would he spend time with him in ICU with Will in a coma? More questions came to mind. Why wasn't his boss at work looking for him? Jack assumed he had a job, but he had no idea what it was. A good boss would look for a missing employee, he reasoned. Maybe he was his own boss, and his employees were too busy trying to keep the business afloat. No, employees would at least report him missing. So would the boss, for that matter. He thought some more about his situation—until the pain got more intense. He looked at the time and noticed he was due for pain medication—just as the nurse walked in with a little cup. Not long afterward, Jack fell asleep.

* * * * *

Jack was seeing two people, but this time he could tell they were male and female. He focused his eyes and recognized Kathy. The guy standing next to her had to be Will. Will thought Jack recognized him. He didn't seem to be as confused as Kathy made him out to be.

"Hi, Jack. Remember me?" It had to be Will, and Will wanted to make sure Jack knew him. Otherwise, he would have to work their conversation from a different angle. Kathy was with him, but she remained quiet.

"You must be Will. I recognize you some, but I'm weak on details. Forgive me. I hope to start remembering more and more as time passes." Kathy was smiling. Jack seemed greatly improved from yesterday.

"I forgot to ask Kathy yesterday," Jack said, turning toward her. "How did you know I was in this hospital?" Kathy and Will told Jack they called every hospital in the city and outlying communities to see if there was a Jack Olsen. They hadn't thought to check the Detroit Medical Center first! They left it until nearly last.

"We would have found you sooner, but we didn't think you would be in the same hospital Will had been in," Kathy said. She was willing for Jack and Will to reestablish their relationship, but she was not willing to step completely out of this conversation.

"Mom and Dad want to come and see you, but they are very busy for the next few days," Kathy added. "They will come as soon as they can. They know you will be here a while."

"I've been asking around here about what happened to me, but no one is telling me much," Jack said. "All I know is that I was brought in on an ambulance, and that I apparently died a few times on the way in. I think they know more, but I must be dealing with people who like to keep secrets. Do you know anything?"

Will took over the conversation. "It looks like God has more for you to do," he said. "Jack, do you know what line of work you were in?" Jack racked his brain, but could not remember.

"By the time we contacted the Detroit Medical Center we had learned a thing or two about how to get information," Will said. "All they told us here was that you came in on an ambulance. We were able to track down the ambulance company and find the medics that brought you in. Are you sure you don't remember what you did for a living?"

"No, I don't. I don't know if I was a business owner, a manager, an employee, or whatever. Believe me, I've tried, but I don't have a clue."

Will paused for a moment, looked down, then continued. "Jack, they found you in the warehouse district, in an alley near an abandoned warehouse. The 911 operator received an anonymous call near morning. The medics estimated that you had been there for several hours. They figured you would surely die before they could get you to the emergency room. It was a day that they will not forget; they used all their training and skills to keep you alive. I had life-threatening injuries when I got beat up, but some of yours were as bad and even worse. I didn't flatline on the way to the emergency room several times—you did."

"Will, even if I could remember other injuries, I think that I would still say that I had never hurt so bad. I think every nerve in my body was working overtime."

Will continued to bring Jack up to date regarding their friendship. Jack was glad they hadn't lost contact with each other. It sounded like Will was a better person than Jack knew himself to be.

"Have you contacted your parents?" Will asked.

"No, I can't do that."

"Why not?"

"I think that I must have left on bad terms or something. I may not have contacted them very much since I've been in Detroit. It wouldn't be right for me to call them now when I didn't bother to keep in touch before. Besides, I'll eventually heal up, and things will get back to normal."

"Normal?" Will asked. "Not keeping in touch with your parents is normal? Your head must have gotten hurt more than we thought." Will smiled, but he meant it to be a serious comment at the same time. Since Will came to Christ, he had learned that honoring one's parents was a priority. He knew it was important to make things right with one's parents before they died. He knew people who didn't learn that lesson, and they were suffering physically, mentally, spiritually, and emotionally because they didn't do it in time.

"Regardless of what went on in your house, I'm willing to bet that your parents are missing you and are worried," Will went on. "Parents don't stop being parents because you move away, and they love you more than you could know."

Jack didn't like what Will was saying. Sure, they might have been friends, but Jack wasn't sure everything Will was saying was right or that Will had the right to say these things to him.

Before he could respond, two policemen entered his room. One looked around briefly, glanced at Will and Kathy, waited for only a few seconds, then spoke up. "Mr. Jack Olsen? We would like to ask you some questions."

In all his time dealing drugs, Jack had never talked with the police.

He had prided himself on being able to slip through their surveillance. Whenever a bust went down, he was always somewhere else. He was aware that they knew of him, but they could not get anything on him. Right now, things were different because he did not remember his past, and he had no idea why the police would come to the hospital to talk to him. Will and Kathy were just as surprised as Jack, and they left the room when asked to do so by the two officers.

"What is this all about, officers?" Jack was trying to make even a small bit of sense of everything.

One of the two stepped forward slightly, seeming to take the lead in questioning Jack. "Mr. Olsen, we are conducting an investigation and have reason to believe that you may have information on the death of an individual named Michael Davidson." Jack could feel his heart skip a beat. *What is going on? Who is this Michael?* And why, Jack asked himself, would they think that he knew this man? On top of that, surely these officers knew that Jack was just now beginning to regain some of his memory. He didn't have anything to say that could help them.

"I don't know this Michael, and I don't know how he could be related to me in anyway. I've been through some major trauma, and I'm just now beginning to remember some things, but I don't remember this guy. Why do you think that I would know him?"

"We don't know what you don't know," the first officer answered. "But we do know that we found Mr. Davidson dead in his car in the Detroit River. It was made to look like an accident, like he had fallen asleep at the wheel late at night and drove into the river. Whoever did it thought we would not be able to find much, but we found enough to determine it wasn't an accident. The forensics lab found evidence of two gunshots. This was a professional hit job. We also found information that led us to you."

Jack took all this in without much emotion—until the moment he realized they were suspecting *him* of being involved in the murder of a person he could not remember.

"What information?"

"We found your name on some papers in a waterproof bag. This is a good time for you to tell us what you know, Mr. Olsen."

"What I know? *What I know?!* I don't know anything. I told you. I can't remember much before last week." Jack's mind was in a whirlwind. Did he kill somebody? Did he help kill somebody? Is this Michael somehow related to Jack's wounds? Why would Jack have reason to kill someone? Did he need a lawyer?

"Look, sirs, I don't know any Michael. And I don't know about any killing. I want you to leave now. I don't have anything to say to you."

"Mr. Olsen, know this," the first officer said. "We have not read you your rights. You still have time to come clean. Should you refuse to cooperate, we think that we will have enough evidence to put you behind bars for a long time once we finish this investigation. Something we haven't told you yet is that you have been under surveillance for a long time. We know of your involvement in the drug trade. We know of your relationship with Jason Miles. We know that you were second in the organization to him, and we believe that you know the inner workings of the organization. There is no way that disappearances like Mr. Davidson's could happen without your knowledge. And yes, we believe we can tie you into the others of which we are aware. So think long and hard. This joy ride is over. We'll be back to talk with you later."

When the officers turned and left the room, Will and Kathy returned. Jack was as pale as a ghost. He didn't notice them entering.

Will spoke first. "Jack, are you OK? What happened? What did they say?"

"They think I killed somebody." Jack told them both what he just went through. All the time, he seemed to stare into space. He said words like someone who had just memorized a script, but wasn't really into delivering it.

Will and Kathy asked him more questions, but Jack only mumbled replies. They could not make out what he was saying except for an occasional mention of someone named Jason. Eventually, Jack mumbled something about being alone, and he rolled over in bed and faced the wall. Will and Kathy thought it wise to cover him up with his sheet and leave him alone for the rest of the day and evening.

Will and Kathy had to tell their parents what happened. They didn't know how they would react. They didn't know how to react themselves. The Jack they knew was incapable of killing someone, but it seemed the police were pretty confident they had enough evidence. Of course, they weren't the final word. First, the district attorney would have to decide to bring charges, and he or she wouldn't do that unless they thought they had enough evidence to bring a conviction in a court of law. Still, the police officers seemed confident.

* * * * *

Later that day when told, Mrs. Williams didn't say anything. She waited for her husband to speak first, and it took a while for him to say anything.

"This looks bad, real bad. If what you say is true, Jack has gotten himself in some serious trouble. Let's assume he is guilty, as they seem to be saying. I don't believe he is unredeemable. Whether he was involved in some criminal activity or not, we will not cast him aside. Each of us has done wrong at some point in our lives, and God still loved us. Each one of us has experienced His unmerited favor. The least we can do is extend grace to one who, like us, doesn't deserve it."

Mrs. Williams asked about contacting Jack's parents. Will and Kathy reminded them that Jack had not kept in touch with his parents, and he didn't want them to see him when he was so badly injured. He would surely not want them to know that he might be guilty of murder.

* * * * *

Back home, life went on as life always does. Susan had missed Jack terribly at first, but eventually she got over him and started dating other guys. If she kept this up, no one would be surprised if she got married within a year or two.

Becky and Susan were good friends. Susan was actually a good influence on Becky. Between Mrs. Olsen and Susan, Becky navigated her high school years with only the occasional bump in the road.

Don was, well, Don. He had a wild streak for a while, having looked up to Jack when he was home. When Jack left, Don began to notice a growing gloominess that his parents seemed to carry about them. It didn't help that Jack communicated so infrequently. Without Don realizing it, he began to set aside his rambunctious ways and became quite responsible for his age. He dated some, but he also made sure he was respectful and avoided doing anything wrong. He would not hurt his parents if he could help it, and he would do his best not to embarrass them.

Mrs. Olsen kept busy. She was active in volunteer activities outside the home, but she also spent a considerable amount of time taking on new beautification projects around the house. One time, she won city Yard of the Month, and was able to display the coveted sign in her yard. But her most rewarding efforts went toward supporting Don and Becky in their activities. She heard other parents complain about all the times they had to go to games and school activities, but these things weren't a burden for her. She looked forward to them. She knew these days would soon pass, and she wanted to have plenty of memories.

Mr. Olsen kept busy with his business. He also enjoyed supporting Don and Becky in their activities. He treated them differently, though. He challenged Don as only a father can. Don's parents decided early on that Don would need more time with his father as he got older, especially after the age of twelve. They had read, and knew well, that boys needed the influence of a father to help them become good men. The age where most cultures started that transition was around twelve. And this is what they focused on doing. Don loved his mother like only boys can, but he spent a lot of time with his dad—fishing, working together in the yard, and sometimes even joining him at his work.

With Becky, although she gravitated toward her mother, Mr. Olsen watched over her like a hawk. He liked to put the fear of God into the boys she dated. There were times he was convinced women just didn't understand the drive to have sex that men had. He remembered how he and his friends were when he was young. Every girl was a target of opportunity, someone to be conquered if given the chance. He knew that wrong, as well as right, decisions could be life-changing. As far as he was concerned, his daughter was going to be kept away from the wrong ones and encouraged to make the right ones. He also wanted to be a good role model for her as to how a man should behave toward his wife, so he made sure he treated his wife like a queen and that Becky noticed.

But even as they lived life together, in their quiet moments all four of them thought often of Jack. How was he doing? Was he safe? Was he making good decisions? Why didn't he call more often? Don, especially, was affected by his absence. He put up a strong facade, but over time, he developed an anger mixed with inner disappointment. More than the others, he kept himself occupied so he wouldn't think about Jack so much.

ELEVEN

A Better Deal

Two traitors in two months. That's how Jason saw it. Mikey first, then Jack. If it hadn't been for Bobby's sharp attention to detail, who knows how much more the organization would have been damaged?

Jason hated to mete out discipline. He saw doing so as, partly, a failure to build a team on his part. But he also saw it as confirmation that people could not be trusted. He would be pulled in two directions. First, he would slump into a depression at his perceived failures. Second, he would become angry and more difficult to be around. It was during these competing states of mind that he was prone to make the worst of decisions.

Bobby knew enough to stay out of Jason's way for a while. Even though he had positioned himself to become the number two man in the organization, he knew he could lose Jason's confidence just as quickly. Bobby was pleased with himself, how he had gotten Jack out of the way. He was pretty sure Jack had died of his injuries considering the state in which they left him in that alley. Now Bobby's task was to walk gently for a while. His ultimate goal was to replace Jason with himself, but he had to bring in his own trusted people.

Margaret noticed Jason's ill humor. It wasn't new to her, but she never could quite figure what was causing it. This time around, she thought she had a clue. Since Jason was not around much, she found herself spending more time studying her Bible and hanging out with Christian friends she had made since she started going to church. Jason didn't know she was going to church. If he found out, he would not be happy. Miriam was still Margaret's mentor. Margaret was so glad the two had met.

Margaret was discovering that Christianity was nothing like she had been led to believe. It was nothing like the secular media made it seem, and even Christian media presented an unbalanced view of what it meant to follow Christ. For most of her life, she viewed Christianity as a group of people who believed in God but had differing views on Jesus. Some thought He was the only way to God, others thought He was one of several ways to God, and still others thought it didn't matter much because a loving God would accept everyone, especially if they spent their lives on earth being good. Their views of Hell and Heaven and eternity were all over the place as well, Margaret had thought. After experiencing Christ personally, the way Miriam explained it, Margaret knew she had to go to a church that was teaching from the Bible; she purchased a study Bible for herself. What she was learning was that much of living this life wasn't as complicated and confusing as she had been led to believe. She concluded that people who had so many odd opinions just didn't spend any time reading the Bible. When they did venture into it, one would view it with modern eyes instead of considering it in its historical and cultural context. Best of all, Margaret was discovering, when she did what it said to do, it worked.

Her whole life was changing in positive ways. Relationships were being healed. She had peace like she never knew before. The difficulties she faced, although still challenging, did not seem impossible. In time, not only did she get more understanding of her faith, she also gained wisdom. Combined, these two things helped her immensely in dealing with and understanding Jason.

Her insight into the cause of Jason's ill temperament came from her Bible study and the counsel of her friend, Miriam. On the one hand, she attributed her personal changes in her relationship with Jason to her new relationship with Christ and her submission to His commands as she discovered them in her studies. On the other hand,

Miriam helped her to see that most of Jason's issues were rooted in his rejection of the claims of Christ.

* * * * *

"You have to serve somebody," Miriam was telling Margaret one day.

"What do you mean?"

"It's not hard. You either serve God or you fill the void with something else."

"Again, what do you mean?"

"Before you came to our church, the pastor preached a sermon where he said that there is a hole in each of us that only Christ can fill. Those who reject Christ try to fill it with other things like money, a job, cars, popularity, sex, and so on. None of those can take the place of Jesus. Even good things cannot fill the void. Ultimately, people end up living lives of quiet desperation."

"That does seem to describe Jason. Since I've known him, he has talked about getting rich and being somebody. He has always complained about people betraying him and how he doesn't trust anybody. Still, he never seems to have any peace about him."

"How has he responded to your accepting Christ?"

"At first, he didn't seem to have much of a reaction, but when he noticed that my life was changing, he began to get angry more often. He also got angry when I would do anything nice for him. It was like he couldn't receive kindness if he thought it came from God through me. Why do you think he reacts that way?"

"It could be any number of things. He could be angry at God. He could be angry with himself and believe he doesn't deserve forgiveness. Sometimes people feel they are so bad that they refuse to forgive themselves even if they accept that God forgives them. In his case, since he doesn't believe in God, he may have put himself between a rock and a hard place. God doesn't forgive him, and he doesn't forgive himself."

"That makes sense," Margaret said. "I always knew deep inside that I was not right with God. When I accepted Jesus, I experienced great relief. Later, I had a similar sensation when I forgave myself. What do you think he is trying to fill the void in his life with?"

"I don't know. Have you ever met any of his coworkers?" Miriam paused, cleared her throat. "Have you been to his workplace? Have you seen his pay stub?"

"You know, I haven't seen any of his friends from work, except Jack, and I've never been to the workplace or seen his pay stub. In fact, if I had an emergency, I wouldn't even know how to get to where he works."

"Margie, when people keep secrets from each other, it usually means they have something to hide." In saying this, Miriam didn't realize how silly it sounded, but it made Margaret think anyway. Why didn't she know more about Jason's work? What was he hiding from her? She would ask him, but he was so on edge lately. She decided she would ask Jack first. They worked at the same place.

Margaret tried for weeks to get in touch with Jack, but he never returned her calls. She didn't know his phone had been thrown in a Dumpster during the savage beating he took. She finally stopped one day and asked Jason about Jack.

"How's Jack doing? I haven't seen or heard from him in weeks."

"He's OK, I guess."

"What do you mean? Don't you see him?"

"Not anymore. He moved on." Jason didn't spend much time trying to polish his lying, so it was easy to see he was hiding something.

"You mean he doesn't work with you anymore? How is it possible that your closest friend leaves and you don't tell me? How is it possible that he leaves and we don't give him some kind of farewell?"

"Oh, he got a farewell," Jason said, looking at her. Jason remembered the night he settled scores with Jack. There was a slight smirk on his face, and Margaret caught it.

"Jason, is he all right? Has something happened to Jack?" Margaret betrayed her concern. She had learned to like Jack. She knew he was turned off by her new faith, but his heart wasn't as hardened as Jason's seemed to be. With those questions, Jason's civility toward Margaret quickly turned.

"How am I supposed to know? It's not my turn to watch him! I'm not his keeper!" Jason was sick and tired of Margaret's badgering and complaining. She wasn't guilty of either, really, but Jason had to convince himself she was so he could justify his rejection of her and his self-rationalization. He stormed from the apartment.

* * * * *

A few days later, Jason came back and began to pack his things. It wasn't the first time their arguing led to his moving out of the apartment.

This time, however, it was different. Margaret was not the insecure, enabling person he knew when he was in jail. When he threatened to leave in the past, or actually did, she would try to keep him there through reasoning, arguing, and finally crying. He always left for a while, sometimes even weeks. But he would return, and things would return to a type of normalcy between them. But this time . . . this time Margaret remained calm and apologized for any part she had played in his decision. She then offered to help him pack. Jason snapped at her to shut up and stay away from him. She stood by as he loaded his car. When he came back for his last things, as if she hadn't already surprised him with her overall reaction, she spoke to him for the last time.

"I'm sorry we were not able to work it out. I hope you find the peace you're looking for." She paused to see his reaction. Jason just stood there, giving nothing away.

Then, as calmly as she could, she said, "Don't expect to come back here. Our relationship is finished."

He could not believe his ears. For a moment, he felt like giving her a piece of his mind—or worse! He didn't need her! He didn't need anybody! There were plenty of women who would give everything to be with him. By the time he started his car, he was fuming. He spent the rest of the day and evening at a nearby bar. He slept that night in one of the abandoned warehouses he liked to use for secret meetings, where the organization had stashed a cot and some blankets. In his drunken sleep, he could hear rats scurrying along the floor. Sometime during the night, he thought he felt one crawl over him. He didn't care. He was *somebody*.

* * * * *

Margaret was as surprised as anyone by her strength and composure. After Jason left, she returned to the apartment and called Miriam.

"Miriam, Jason just moved out."

"Really?" Miriam was trying to control her joy at hearing this news.

"Yes. He'd been acting strange, moody, and introverted—more than normal. I got tired of trying to contact Jack, so I asked him about it. I knew it could result in an argument, but I feel he knows something."

"Did he tell you anything?"

"He said that Jack had moved on. Can you believe it? He wouldn't have said anything to me. I had to ask. That doesn't look right from any direction."

"Jack is gone? We didn't even know he was thinking of leaving. It would have been nice to have given him a farewell party."

"That's what I told Jason. He just came back with something about Jack did get a proper farewell. What does that mean? It sounds weird. When I pressed him on it, he got defensive and angry. He left and then came back today and started packing his stuff to move out."

"What did you do?"

"I apologized for whatever part I had in his decision, and I offered to help him pack. That really riled him up, and he told me to stay away from him. So I just stood by and watched. You know, just telling you about it now makes me see the humor in it."

Miriam was intrigued by this last statement. Jason and Margaret had been together a good while. He would sometimes get angry and move out, but he would always come back like nothing happened. This was different in some way, and Miriam thought she knew why.

"How long do you think he will stay away this time before he comes back?"

"He won't be coming back. I told him our relationship was through, and he wouldn't be moving back in. In fact, I'm going to change the locks to make sure he can't get in if I'm not home." Margaret didn't know it, but that last part caused Miriam to sit down. "I also told him that I hope he will find peace."

"Wow! *Wow!*" Miriam almost couldn't contain herself. "What happened next? Did he say or do anything?"

"He didn't say anything. He just got in the car and left."

"Wow. How do you feel?"

"Believe it or not, it's a relief. I could see this coming. I've really become serious about following Christ. The more I read the Bible and the more I pray, I can see that our living arrangement was wrong, and that I was unequally yoked with an unbeliever."

"Margie, I'm glad for you. What you did took courage. Now, I don't want to take away from your joy. But I want you to know that this is a loss in your life. People grieve differently. Right now, your initial reaction is happiness, probably because you proved to yourself that you are stronger than you thought. But don't be surprised if you find yourself crying later. It's perfectly normal."

Margie took it all in. She trusted Miriam. Miriam was a source of great wisdom and counsel, so she thanked her for being there, for being so patient with her when she was struggling to understand.

Miriam proved to be right. A few days later, Margaret found herself crying for no apparent reason. But she knew exactly why. She was grieving for the loss of the relationship and also for Jason's rejection of Christ.

* * * * *

Bobby looked in the mirror. He was looking at the next big shot in the Greater Detroit area drug trade. He smiled. He considered changing his hairstyle and growing a beard, maybe a goatee. He would certainly have to improve his wardrobe. He couldn't go around looking like a worker bee or middle management. Yes sir, he was going to be top dog. His preparations were almost complete.

When he was finished, Jason wouldn't know what hit him.

It helped that Jason had split up with Margaret. Jason thought he was always in control, but when things weren't stable in his life, Jason didn't know what to do. In other words, he was not good at calming things down. If anything, he would destabilize the situations in his life even more. His life was as unstable as Bobby had seen in their time together. Jason liked to think he didn't need anybody, but he was so wrong. He actually had depended on Margaret a lot. Even though she had become a Christian—maybe because of it—she had brought a steadiness to their life together that he couldn't capture on his own.

In truth, Jason was very unsure of himself. He tried to move back in with Margaret, but she stood firm in her decision. He refused to beg and tried to act like he was angry—but really, he was scared. He didn't realize how much she meant to him until he lost her.

Margaret, on the other hand, was able to move on. She had good people around her, a good church, and was gaining a confidence she never had before. She was looking forward to the future, and she knew that her future would include Jesus. She learned in her studies that He promised to never leave her. And now He had proven His reliability in enough ways that Margaret fully believed He would keep his word.

Bobby had been busy. As part of his plan, he had become a police informant. He reasoned that he would give them enough information to bring Jason down, but not enough to eliminate the organization. This was going to be easy. It was only a matter of time.

But Bobby had some of the same weaknesses as Jason. He was overconfident in his abilities and insecure at the same time. With his role as an informant, he was the former. He just "knew" that the police weren't smart enough to catch him in his plan to replace Jason. The truth was different. The police, of course, had other informants in the organization. They had infiltrated George's operation and had regular contact with others in the chain. Some of the people that Bobby trusted to help him take over were actually undercover cops. Bobby would laugh as he tried to play both sides against each other. What he didn't know was that the joke was about to be on him.

While all this was going on, Jason decided that now was the time to expand once again. He and Bobby would plan how they would make this move. They couldn't expand the same way they used to when Jack was in the loop, because Jack was the one with the creative ideas, and he was no longer with them. They would have to come up with a different plan on their own. They invited George—or Georgie, as they had now taken to calling him—to join them since he was doing well in his part of town. Georgie appreciated the chance to show them he could rise to the occasion.

"Who is going to take over the new territory?" Georgie asked in one meeting. He wanted to know if these were people he could work with.

"We haven't decided yet," Jason said. "We got some names, but we're still checking them out. Some are relatively new. I hate to promote new guys too soon, but with our recent losses, coupled with our growth, we're forced to take some chances."

What Jason didn't know was that some of the newer people he was considering were undercover police officers. The three of them were doing the work for the police and didn't even know it. Bobby, especially, was clueless and overconfident. Georgie just wanted to prove himself to the other two.

So Jason found himself in a new reality. Jack, who had been with him from the start, was gone and, to his knowledge, probably dead. Margaret had left him. But even this wasn't true; it wasn't as Jason saw it in his mind. *He* was the one who left her. The fact that Margaret wouldn't take him back convinced him that she left him. It was an interesting twisting of the facts that he used to protect his frail ego. Nothing could ever be Jason's fault. Now he was surrounded with people in important roles who had not gained his trust. He would be forced to make more decisions on his own. Those would bring him closer to his downfall.

* * * * *

Bobby set up a sudden buy. He was able to sell Jason on it because the price was so low. In earlier times, Jack would have cautioned against a buy like this because it seemed too good to be true. But Jason didn't have the benefit of Jack's counsel anymore, and in his mind, a low price was a good deal. It couldn't be too good to be true because Jason was worthy of the best deal, and such a deal fit his criteria. But it was a trap. Bobby was ready to make his play. He had set Jason up so that he would be caught making the buy. The police would have everything they needed to put him away for a long time. Bobby would make sure Jason had a large amount of cash on him, and there would be a lot of drugs present. This was just too easy, Bobby thought. With Jason out of the way, he would be the logical one to succeed him. He already had bought off any potential competition.

The plan was for Jason, Bobby, and Georgie to be taken into custody at the same time. After all three were taken to jail, Bobby would be released without the knowledge of the other two. What Bobby didn't know was that when the police took the three of them in, he would not be released as he thought. He would be booked with the two of them and charged with the same crimes. The police were making a wide sweep of drug dealers that day with the intent of slowing down, if not altogether stopping, the drug trade in the southeast corner of Michigan and in Greater Detroit.

* * * * *

As it played out, it became a scene out of a gangster movie. Several vehicles came from different directions. As they got closer, Jason, Bobby, and George dimmed their lights just enough to see what was going on in front of them, but not so much as to attract more attention. From two places in the dark, two men in heavy coats walked into view. Once they were in place, the seller—who was actually an undercover cop—stepped out of the back of another vehicle and slowly made his way forward to a spot equal distance from the two men. They were also undercover police, and there was more backup available if needed. They each had a panic button sewn into their coats. If only one of them pressed it, the entire place would fill with police.

From the other side, a single car approached at the appointed time. It too dimmed its lights as it got closer. Two men got out of the back seat, one on each side of the car. They walked forward a short distance, and then one of them stopped. The other continued moving toward to the seller. They shook hands, and the seller showed him some of the product. The one who walked forward was Georgie. He sniffed and tasted the white powder, then nodded his approval. He turned and went back to the car, where Jason was sitting.

"Jason, it's the real deal."

"Are you sure? How do you know the rest of it isn't ground-up white chalk?" Georgie could not believe his ears. This deal was too big for someone to try a stunt like that. Jason always got skittish when it came to closing a deal. That's why he rarely went out himself to buy product. He always sent someone else. And this, he thought, gave him a layer of protection if something went wrong.

"C'mon, man! We've dealt with these guys before," Georgie said, impatiently. "It's always good stuff. If we don't buy it, they'll sell it to someone else, and then we'll just have more competition."

One thing Jason did not like was competition. He nodded at Georgie. Georgie could see that Jason seemed ready to go through, and not to back out at the last minute.

"All right. Let's do it." Jason slowly exited the car and moved forward to meet the seller. After brief introductions, they got down to business.

"My guy says you have the stuff." Jason knew how to intimidate, but the seller didn't seem one to intimidate easily.

"Do you have the money?"

"Show me the stuff one more time." Jason sniffed and tasted it, like Georgie had done before. Georgie was getting anxious. This was getting way more complicated than it needed to be. If they stayed much longer, they could be discovered by the wrong people.

In the meantime, Bobby was standing where he had stopped when the two of them got out of the car. Of all times, he needed to go to the bathroom.

The conversation between Jason and the seller continued a while longer. Jason looked at the full load in the seller's trunk, and he showed him the money. Each assured the other that everything was as it should be. Jason stood there for what seemed an eternity without saying anything. The seller challenged him.

"Are you a cop?"

"Sure. I sell drugs on the side to make ends meet." Jason smiled on the outside. He was sure—at least hoping—this guy knew he was kidding.

"What about you? Are you a cop?" Jason was asking the seller. Georgie and Bobby couldn't believe this conversation was happening. Any minute now, someone was going to get antsy and start shooting. They nervously looked around to make sure no one made any sudden moves. And all the while, Bobby's bladder was screaming.

"If I am, I should get fired," the seller answered. "I can't even make a drug deal."

But Jason felt something funny, and was about to walk away when Georgie approached him and spoke in his ear. Jason looked at the seller one more time.

"OK, you got a deal," Jason said. "This stuff better be good through and through."

"Hey—guaranteed." The product was transferred to Jason's car, and Jason handed the briefcase with the money to the seller.

But the seller wasn't quite done. "You know what else I guarantee?"

"What's that?" Jason huffed.

"I guarantee that you are under arrest."

Immediately, lights came on, and police were swarming the area. *"Down! On your stomachs!* Feet and hands spread where we can see them! Now! Now! *Now!"* The taking down of Jason, Bobby, and Georgie took less time than it took for Jason to take the bait. As nervous as Jason had been to make the deal, he was now extraordinarily calm. He had obviously been arrested before. Georgie, on the other hand, had never experienced anything like this. He was shaking, scared.

And Bobby? The one with his own deal with police? The one who was going to replace Jason at the top? That Bobby? He peed his pants.

On the way to the jail, Officer Pierson, who turned out to be the undercover agent who pretended to be the seller, asked Jason a simple question.

"What did Georgie say in your ear right before you agreed to the buy?"

Jason sneered. "He said I couldn't get a better deal."

TWELVE

Light Breaks Through

Kathy's feelings were all over the place. She did not like that she had fallen for a person who was possibly guilty of murder. She should have known not to let that happen. After all, there was no indication that Jack had any real relationship with God. He always deflected the conversation when the subject of Jesus was brought up. She was glad she didn't let her feelings be known to him, but she was disappointed in herself nevertheless. She was wrestling between rejecting him outright and trying to help him get through whatever was coming. She chose to try to help, mainly because her father had stated that the family would not cast Jack aside. But she promised herself she would be more disciplined.

Will reacted much better. He was actually very compassionate toward Jack. He certainly could relate to the physical pain. As far as Jack's trouble with the law, he would wait and see.

Jack spent several days without a visit from anyone. The James family just got overcome by events in their own lives, so it wasn't until later in the week that Will was able to visit Jack. He was curious to find out if anything had developed with the police, as well as seeing how Jack was doing physically and emotionally.

Jack spent those days doing a lot of thinking. Some of his memory was coming back, and he was pretty sure he had been involved in illegal drug dealing. If that was true, then it was very possible he was guilty of killing someone. This was not good. The police had not come by with any more questions, but he wondered if he needed a lawyer. When he thought about it, which was most of the time, he got depressed. There were still pieces missing in his mind, but this was so serious that he imagined himself spending the rest of his life in prison, or maybe even receiving the death penalty. He didn't even know if Michigan had the death penalty.

It was during one of these melancholy moments that Will came to visit. Jack didn't notice until Will was standing next to his bed.

"Wow, Jack. You seem to be here physically, but you are far away otherwise. How are you feeling?" It was the best way Will knew to start the conversation. He had no idea what he was going to say just a few minutes before walking in Jack's room.

"Oh, sorry. I didn't see you," Jack said. "I'm doing OK, I guess. The pain is starting to subside, and I'm getting more of my memory back every day. Where have you been? In fact, where has everyone been? I thought you all decided to get as far away from me as possible."

"No, it was nothing like that," Will said. "Really, it was just a lot of things that needed tending to. Mom and Dad plan to come by tomorrow, and Kathy might be here tonight or tomorrow sometime." Will paused and seemed to look a bit closer at Jack. "You're looking a bit better. Have you heard anything more from the police?"

"No. Not at all. It's weird. They come in here accusing me of killing someone, and then they disappear. It's like they fell off the edge of the earth. I thought about calling them, but I don't really have anything to tell them."

Will and Jack continued catching up on the latest events, and trying to help Jack with his memory. Will told him more of how they met, and the plans they once had. He told him how he let his friend down when Jack first came to Detroit. The job that Jack thought he was going to have waiting for him didn't materialize, and their plans to share an apartment went down the drain as well.

"I imagine I wasn't happy with those developments."

"No, you weren't. We both moved in with my parents, which was all right with me, but you and my mother did not get along. Eventually you left and got a place of your own, even though it wasn't as nice as my folk's house. You just had to get away from Mom."

"So why is she so nice to me now?" Jack asked. "It seems to me that your whole family treats me better than I treat myself. If there was so much conflict, what happened to change that?"

Will quickly prayed in his mind that he would not blow this second opportunity to tell Jack about how the family came to put their trust in Christ.

"Jack, I've told you this story before. I guess you can't remember it because of your amnesia."

"So tell me again. Maybe it will help me remember other stuff."

Will told him how the family seemed, to the outside world, to be pretty together. Living with them, though, Jack got to see that their day-to-day existence was not as it seemed. They weren't super dysfunctional, but they had issues. Some would say they were a normal family. However, each of them knew, individually, that something was not right. For instance, Dad snapped at people over minor things, and Mom knew how to hold a grudge. Kathy struggled with keeping friends. She was very smart, but couldn't figure out why people avoided her.

The change, Will told Jack, started when his mother "got religion." Will explained to him that his mother had a Christian friend in her art club. Her friend wasn't pushy, but her life displayed a quality that intrigued his mom. She told Will later that she appreciated her friend talking more about Christ with her actions than with words. She was tired of make-believe Christians who could talk a good talk but couldn't back up their words with action. Will filed that information away because he had not yet made a decision to follow Christ.

His father and sister made decisions for Christ soon after his mom, and everything changed. Will could feel it and see it in the way the family related to each other and to others they interacted with. There were no more concerns about Will taking over the company. They recognized that Will's strengths lay elsewhere, and they were fine with that. Kathy, although not entirely sold on taking over the company, was more aware that she had the skill set for it should she decide to go in that direction.

Will didn't know it at the time, but he was experiencing God's love.

This was God's love through others. As he considered the family he once knew and the family he now saw, he became more aware of his own insufficiency. He had been raised to believe that you had to make your way in the world the best you can. That was now being challenged by the changes he saw in his family. There was more peace, for example. God was now in charge.

Will did not come to Christ as soon as his family. He did some research and compared other religions with Christianity. He hoped he could find some medical or scientific reasons for the changes he was seeing. As he tried to disprove his family's faith, he kept coming across the one fact he couldn't disregard. That was the resurrection of Jesus Christ. No other religion boasted of a resurrected Savior. Another thing he experienced was a sense of guilt. He knew some called it sin. He knew enough from his upbringing that there was such a thing. "You never have to teach a child how to do wrong," he would hear people say. Human nature leans toward evil. Eventually, Will prayed for forgiveness and asked Jesus to be the Lord of his life.

"I could tell you more, but there's not enough time to tell you what's happened since I asked Jesus to take over."

Jack did not reject him, and surprisingly did not interrupt him one time during Will's sharing of this recent past.

"You almost got killed for being a Christian." Jack said it with a tone that combined admiration with a question.

"Yes, but the Bible says that they persecuted Jesus, and they will also persecute us. It also says that Jesus came to give us life, and more abundant life. So it's not all one or the other. It's both."

Jack took it all in but didn't say anything more. Their conversation turned to Will asking about Jack's parents, how things were going back home. He knew that Jack didn't keep in touch with his family.

But before he could pursue that avenue of discussion, police officers entered the room.

Jack was visibly concerned, even fearful. Since nobody asked him to leave, Will stayed in the room to see what was going to happen.

"Mr. Olsen, how are you today? You look a little pale, but surely you must be healing up," an officer said.

Jack muttered something about how he was feeling better. But he realized he was just filling the air with words, hoping that he wasn't going to hear bad news.

"Well, we might as well get to the point. Do you know a person named Jason Miles?"

"Yes."

"How about a Georgie?"

Jack nodded.

"Bobby?"

"Yes. Why?"

"We knew you did. You know what else we know?" The lead officer was on a roll now. "We know that you were involved with them in running the biggest drug ring in this part of the state."

This was not going in a good direction. Jack's memory wasn't good enough to remember whether what they were saying was true. But he feared they were right. He hoped they couldn't see his body shaking.

"Now, here is something that we know, but you don't know. The reason you don't know is because it happened while you were in here. Do you care to take a guess?"

Before Jack could try to respond, the officer answered his own question. "All three of your friends, plus a bunch of other mid-level and lower-level workers, are in jail. Isn't that something? Here you have the biggest drug ring around, and you're not smart enough to keep it from being infiltrated by narcs. You guys weren't as smart as you thought you were."

Jack learned that his three former business associates had been taken down during a drug deal that was basically a setup by police. What was worse, they were all turning on each other, claiming that they were only a small part of the operation. They pointed to one person as the ringleader: Jack Olsen.

Jack couldn't believe his ears. If he was involved with this group at a high level, their turning on him showed he was not in good standing with them. Was it somehow related to the beating he experienced? He didn't have to wait long for the answer.

"And what we know, and what they don't know, is that you are alive. Yes, we knew about the beating you took. Nothing like a well-placed informant to give a clearer picture. By the time it was over, they were pretty sure that you were either dead, or at death's door, and would just be a memory soon, just like Mikey."

"Why did they try to kill me?"

"Bobby had it in for you and Jason, especially when Georgie got Mikey's old territory. His ultimate plan was to replace you and Jason, but the Georgie deal pushed him over the top, and he decided to act sooner. You were first on his list. Bobby convinced Jason that you were cooking the books and skimming more than you were supposed to. That's why you almost lost your life. Then he set his sights on removing Jason. In Bobby's hurry to remove him, he made a lot of mistakes, which gave away his plan, and helped us break the whole organization."

It was worse than Jack thought. Maybe it would have been better if he had died from the beating. He had never spent any time in prison and didn't have the slightest idea how he would survive in such an environment. If he was convicted of murder, he imagined other convicts would test him to see how tough he really was. He was overwhelmed by fear.

Jack's next statement was simple, to the point, and sounded pretty much like a confession.

"Is there anything good in all of this for me?"

"Maybe. You might not have killed Mikey, at least not directly. We found some email traffic and text messages that seem to exonerate you from that. It seems it was a contract killing, and we believe you didn't know about it."

"That's a relief! I didn't think I killed anyone."

"Not so fast. Just because you might not have killed him, it doesn't mean that you won't be convicted of it in a court of law. Remember that I said that your three amigos were turning on each other and fingering you as the top man? They might be saying this because they believe that you died, but when they find out that you are still alive, they may stick to their story, and then it will be up to a jury to decide who to believe. The jury will have to consider not only the evidence, but who has the most to lose. That would be you. If they are convinced that you were the leader of the group, under the law, you could be convicted of murder even if you didn't actually do it. At the very least, you could be convicted of accessory to murder, and that alone would put you away for a very long time."

"Am I under arrest?"

"Not yet. But you will be as soon as we sort out the paperwork. In the meantime, we don't think you'll be leaving the hospital soon, and we suggest you get yourself a lawyer."

Jack wasn't dying, but he could see what little he remembered of his life pass before his eyes. All this time, Will didn't say anything. When the police left, Will offered to find a lawyer for Jack. Jack didn't know what to do. He didn't even know if he had any money to pay a lawyer. Will told him they would cross that bridge when they got to it.

* * * * *

Jack hardly got any sleep that night, and neither Kathy nor her parents visited the next day. He wondered why, but he had too much on his mind to think much about it.

For the first time, in the quietness of the hospital room, he considered God. This was way too big for him to handle. Maybe that's what people do when they are overwhelmed, Jack thought—turn to their idea of God. Whether that was the case or not, he remembered some of the times he spent with Miriam and Margie, and the stories they told about their turning to God, and what it all meant to them. He vaguely remembered that he blew them off, yet felt a nagging insistence that they were more right than he was. In recent days, he had just learned about Will and his family's experience. Jack always felt that he could win an argument or a debate, but he was at a loss when confronted with an argument backed by an experience. The people in his recent past had similar arguments and similar experiences. It didn't make sense—and yet it made the most sense.

* * * * *

Jack didn't sleep much for two days. On the third night, as he was looking up at the ceiling, he heard himself talking to God. Or perhaps he was just thinking loudly. In any case, no one heard him if he was indeed speaking out loud.

"God, I don't know if you're out there or in here or somewhere. I don't even know if you really exist. But if you do, I'm willing to give you a chance with my life. I've certainly messed it up. You couldn't do any worse than I have."

That felt weird. They used to put people in mental hospitals for thinking they were talking to God.

"I'm sorry for the mess I've made," Jack went on. "I don't want to lie here and try to make a deal with you. None of this, 'Help me out of this mess, and I'll serve you forever.' If you do help me out of this mess, I'll be grateful, is all that I can say."

He stopped for a moment. He didn't think he was making any sense. Did he believe in God or not? Did he believe he was a sinner or not? Did he believe any of this stuff? He tried to speak again, but felt himself choking up and tears forming in his eyes.

Suddenly, he heard himself saying, "Fix me, Lord. Fix me! I'm broke! I need fixing!" Jack instinctively knew that he wasn't talking about his physical condition, which certainly needed help as well. It was something deeper. He had never felt this way, but he knew he was talking about his spiritual condition, about his relationship with a God he wasn't even sure was real. He didn't know how to say it; the words wouldn't come. It seemed like his prayer was coming from deep inside him, as if from heart to heart.

Jack didn't know what was happening. It seemed like a mixture of remorse, repentance, and joy all blended together. His tears were coming freely now, and he found himself gulping, as a drowning man seeks air. He would later say that it felt like he was being washed. At the end of it all—how long it took, he couldn't tell—he felt clean, cleaner than he had ever felt. His mind was clear, and it seemed he could remember nearly everything. His amnesia seemed gone.

* * * * *

The next day, both Will and Kathy came to visit. The entire James family had been praying for Jack, and they had put his name on a prayer chain at their church, so there were possibly hundreds of people praying for him. Will told his parents and Kathy what the police had said, so they were concerned not only about Jack's future, but also about how he was taking it all. He had spent considerable time at the hospital, first in the ICU and then in a room. He had only partially recovered his memory, his physical wounds were healing slower than expected, and this newest development of his involvement in crime would be too much for most people to bear.

So Will and Kathy came to visit him together. They did so to support each other as much as to deal with Jack. It was good they came together. What they found shocked them.

Jack was sitting in his bed reading a Bible. They had never seen him do that. And he was crying. They had never seen him do that, either. And he was laughing! How was that possible? They didn't know there was anything funny in the Bible.

Jack looked up at them from his reading, eyes swollen from all the crying and a huge smile on his face.

"Hey! Hi! So glad to see you! I've missed you. Where have you been?"

Will and Kathy didn't know how to respond. Will finally got some words out. "Glad to see you, too. Where have you been?"

Will didn't mean it to be funny, but Jack burst out laughing again. "Man, I've got so much to tell you. You might say I went back to my right mind."

Jack went on to tell them about his last few nights, how he considered what Will had said about the changes in his family. He told them that he remembered some friends he had before who told him similar things. Anyway, in his despair over what he was facing, he turned to God and prayed some disjointed, seemingly unbelieving prayer. This resulted in what he could only describe as floodgates opening and a tsunami of love and forgiveness washing over him. He apologized because he couldn't really describe it, but he knew that God was real. Jack continued to try to explain what happened to him. He would talk for a bit, and then start crying, and then start laughing. This went on for a while. Will and Kathy were smiling. They knew what had happened, so they were relieved and happy for Jack. They were also entertained as they let him talk and cry and laugh.

Will had found a lawyer, but Jack decided against using him. He reasoned that his life was not his own anymore, that it belonged to God, and it was God's responsibility to do with him as He wished. He figured that if he went to prison, God would take care of him there. Will and Kathy were a little surprised with his understanding of biblical truth from Scripture he could not have yet read. It was like the Holy Spirit was revealing truth to him that he would later confirm through his Bible reading. Will and Kathy came to see him fearing what they might find, and they left rejoicing at what God had done.

* * * * *

Jack settled into enjoying his visits from the Jameses. The family worked to free up their schedules so that they were visiting him pretty regularly, and Mrs. James treated him like her own son. Mr. James took it upon himself to help Jack with his understanding of Christian discipleship. Either Will or Kathy would visit each day, after they got off work, and on the weekends.

Meanwhile, it seemed that Jack's decision to forego a lawyer was paying off. When Jason, Bobby, and Georgie heard that he had not died, they struck a plea bargain with the district attorney's office. Independent of each other, they were willing to testify that Jack was not involved in the death of Mikey, and in order to avoid life without parole for themselves, they were willing to tell the authorities who did kill Mikey. What they would face, however, would be life in prison, with a chance for parole after thirty years. Jack was still at risk for being charged with drug trafficking, but for some unknown reason, the DA decided not to charge him. Maybe they had bigger fish to fry. As it turned out, Jack did not get off scot-free. He had to serve one thousand hours of community service and promised to inform on other dealers he knew about. Plus, he was put on three years' probation. One little slipup with the law, and he would most likely join his former business partners in prison for a long time. Still, this was better than he expected. Before, Jack would not have believed this turn of events was possible. Now he was amazed and thankful for God's mercy.

The Way Up

* * * * *

As each day passed, Jack realized he had never seen a better day. That's how he began his answer to people whenever they would ask how he was doing: "I've never seen a better day." And it was true. He immersed himself in Bible study and was learning to pray. He actually felt the presence of God in a stronger way than he thought possible. He was eventually released from the hospital and accepted an offer to stay with the Jameses until he got on his feet. After all, he was no longer doing what he had been doing before. *This is what a honeymoon must feel like,* he would say to himself.

All honeymoons come to an end, however. It started when Jack read in his Bible, "Honor your father and mother . . . " He didn't think anything of it the first time he read those words, but they planted themselves deeply within him. It would only be a matter of time before they would grow enough to get his attention.

There were other things going on that troubled him. He was getting less and less immediate answers to prayer, and he was thinking more about making things right with people from his past. This ran counter to what he had come to understand about following Jesus. After coming to Christ, he had done a lot of reading apart from the Bible as well as from the Scriptures themselves. He had assumed that if something was Christian, it had to be good. He was grateful for all the good things he learned, but he was beginning to see that he had to be more discerning about what he accepted as truth. Just because it was written on a Christian website or publication didn't mean it was true, or good. And he didn't really see it written anywhere, but at some point he began to believe that if a person accepted Christ, his life would become better and better. It was almost like God was some kind of sugar daddy. Although he knew that wasn't true, he had begun to act like he expected his life to be trouble free.

Later Jack would say this process is like when a baby is weaned from the bottle and starts eating more solid foods. God was doing the same with him. Spiritually, He was taking Jack off the bottle and pushing him to eat solid food. It really clicked when he remembered that Will had been beaten for his faith in Christ. Together with some

Scriptures he had read about being persecuted, he realized that the Christian life was not meant to be trouble free. He smiled when he realized how obvious it was, and how he had missed it.

Jack's growth in his Christian faith happened most when he found time to be quiet and alone. For him, it was usually early in the morning, before everyone got up and started their day. Once in a while, it would happen in the middle of the night. When that happened, he would usually stay up the rest of the night praying and taking notes. He actually did not mind being tired the next day for lack of sleep. Those times of receiving revelation from God in the middle of the night were precious to Jack. A few times, he forced himself to wake up on his own so he could study and pray, but nothing happened that was noteworthy. He learned that if God didn't wake him, he might as well enjoy his sleep.

It was totally different one night. He woke up, and he could sense something was different. He knew enough to recognize when he was being spiritually attacked. This was not that. He felt a heaviness in the air. He wondered what God was trying to tell him. And then it came: "Honor your father and mother." He couldn't tell if he heard an audible voice or if he remembered this from his earlier readings. The Jameses were like another set of parents to him. They had gone out of their way to help him when he was at his most needy. Their faith walk encouraged him. He tried to honor them the best he could.

And yet that feeling, that deep sense of something he was being called to, would not go away. ". . . so that it may go well with you and that you may enjoy long life on the earth." Those words are also part of the same verse, the one about honoring parents! Jack wondered why he hadn't remembered them before. *What was God trying to say?* he would ask himself.

"Honor *your* father and mother . . . so that it may go well with *you* and that *you* may enjoy long life on the earth."

Jack remembered that he once heard at church that life isn't about yourself, it is all about God. Well, that seemed to conflict with what he was hearing now, because these words from God were emphasizing Jack's parents and Jack's life. His biological parents were still alive. This was another of those times when Jack was uncomfortable with the direction things were going. If he was hearing correctly, he needed to honor his parents—the ones he hardly kept in touch with, the ones who resisted his leaving home.

It was one thing to make restitution with people from outside the family, but this was different. How would he honor them from a distance? Somehow he knew honoring them from a distance was not what God wanted. Jack was not writing any notes now. He deliberately quit thinking about his parents and fell asleep.

THIRTEEN

The U-Turn

Don was not happy with the way things had turned out. His brother wasn't as nice as he thought him to be when he was younger, and it really ticked him off that Jack wouldn't keep in touch. Don could see his mother aging and the frown lines on his father getting deeper. They would never say anything negative about Jack, but he knew they were hurt badly by his lack of communication. His sister, Becky, confided in Don some. She was angry, too, but not as much as he. She wanted to believe that Jack would return one day with stories of daring exploits and successes he experienced when he went out on his own. He had probably invested his college money that he got when he left home, and was probably, at that moment, living like a king. In any case, she reasoned, there likely was a good reason why Jack didn't call or write or text or email. The more Becky thought about it, it did seem a little too much to believe, but she had a way of dancing her way through difficult moments and things she didn't want to confront.

One thing was for certain in Don's mind. If he ever saw Jack again, he would give him a piece of his mind. It didn't matter how good his reasons for not keeping in touch, they would not excuse him. The others might not say anything, but he would, by God.

Jack's parents did spend time discussing what, if anything, they should do. After losing contact following Jack's first few stops in Detroit, they once considered putting in a missing persons report, but this seemed a bit much, so they thought better of that option. They thought of going to Detroit and looking for him, but they didn't know where they would start. They had no address for him. Also, Mr. Olsen just couldn't see himself taking time off work. The business greatly depended on him being there.

Don overheard a friend tell his father that Jack just needed to find himself, that this was a phase many young people go through. Although Don was not yet on his own, he thought that was one of the dumbest things he ever heard. You don't kick your family to the curb in order to "find yourself." He heard his father graciously respond to the man: "One thing is for sure. He needs to be found."

* * * * *

Meanwhile, Jack's overwhelming experience with God in the hospital had given way to bouts with depression. It wasn't noticeable to anyone else, but at night he would lie in bed, feeling guilt and remorse over the way he left home and had treated his family since. He didn't know what he should do. For sure, he thought, his family had disowned him by now. He had wasted the money his father had given him, and he didn't have one college credit hour to his name. Not to mention that his original plans hadn't worked out, and he had fallen in with a dangerously bad crowd, almost costing him his freedom and his life. In short, when Jack thought about it, if there was someone who messed up his life worse than him, he didn't know who it would be. If he did go home, he would really have to humble himself and accept that his parents might totally reject him. He did not know if he could stand such complete humiliation and rejection.

One night in the quiet of his bedroom, Jack simply never fell asleep. He started thinking about how he had lived his life since leaving home, the changes he experienced, and the biggest change of his life up to now. He gradually became sadder and sadder, until he silently began to weep. The guilt and shame became overwhelming when he once again thought about his family. "Honor your father and mother . . . ." The phrase kept coming to him. Every time, he would cry a little harder, hurt a little deeper.

He knew what he had to do.

It was a Saturday morning. Usually everyone slept in on Saturday. That meant that Jack had to wait even longer for the James family to make their way down for what passed for breakfast on the weekend. Each family member made their own; often it was just cereal and fruit. Jack cleaned himself up as best as he could. He knew that Mrs. James, especially, would say something if she knew he hadn't slept all night. He didn't know how they would react to what he was going to tell them. The more he thought about it, the harder it became for him. When he was sure all of them were there, he made his way to the kitchen.

"Good morning, Jack. Why, you're dressed all spiffy this morning." Leave it to Mr. James to notice how he was dressed and completely miss the dark bags under his eyes.

"Good morning, sir." This felt like when he approached his own father about leaving home. *This kind of thing never gets easier,* Jack thought.

Will's mom was busy getting coffee and juice for everyone, so she was distracted enough that she didn't notice that Jack had been crying and surely hadn't gotten a full night's sleep. Will and Kathy, on the other hand, could see that something was up. In a low voice, Will just whispered to Jack, "Whoa, dude." Before he could say anything else, Jack started to say what he came to say.

"I'm glad you're all here together, because I have something to say that I wouldn't want to have to say four separate times."

"What? What is it, dear? Did you go without sleep again?" Mrs. James finally noticed, but now she was interested in what he was about to say, so she decided to forego her concern about his lack of sleep until later.

Kathy briefly jumped in. "What is it? You getting married?" She felt stupid as soon as she said it. She hoped they couldn't see her face, red with embarrassment.

"Let him talk. Go ahead," Mr. James said. "Whatever it is, it must be important." He could see that Jack had thought long and hard about what he was going to say, and he wanted to hear it, if only to help Jack get it off his chest.

Jack began again. "I've been thinking about what I've been reading in the Bible. I don't want to be one of those people who claims to be a Christian, but you can't tell it by their actions. It seems to me that some people would prefer to be undercover Christians. They don't want anyone to know. It's like they're embarrassed or afraid of what someone might think. You aren't like that, and I don't want to be like that."

"OK. So what's your point?" It was Will, who wasn't making it any easier for Jack to say what he was trying to say.

"Well, I've been thinking that if I am truly going to be a follower of Christ, then I need to do what He wants me to do, as far as I can determine what His will is."

"It sounds like some of that Bible is sticking to you," Mr. James said. "What are you going to do? Become a missionary?" He thought he was trying to help Jack focus, and Jack appreciated it, but this wasn't what he was trying to say.

"No, not in the traditional sense. I feel like I have to do some things before I can even begin to imagine how God might use or bless me in the future. I've hurt a lot of people. I've tried to make things right with the ones I could find, but some still remain."

Before he could continue, Mrs. James chimed in. "That's just wonderful. We're so glad you are serious about your faith. Now, what is it with you not sleeping very much lately? Just look at you. Your eyes are all red and swollen. You have bags under your eyes. Have you been crying again? Mercy, you are going to have to get ahold of yourself."

That began an exchange between her and Will. Will could tell that Jack wasn't finished, and that his mother had allowed her nurturing instincts to engage her mouth at the wrong time. Finally, Will's mom gave in and spoke directly to Jack.

"Fine! I'm sorry if I cut you off. You know I love you and I worry about you like I do my own children. Now, tell us what you're trying to say!"

"I, uh, I . . . I want to go home."

"What? Honey, you are home." Mrs. James still didn't get it.

"I mean, *home* home. Back south where my birth family is. I haven't seen them for three years, and I haven't talked to any of them for half of that time. I didn't leave under the best of circumstances, and I know they have been worried about me. Who knows, they've probably disowned me by now. I was reading where it says to honor your mother and father, and I can't get it out of my mind. If I'm going to be a faithful disciple of Christ, I've got to at least try to reach out to them. That's why I can't sleep! That's why I cry all the time!" Jack sat down with his face in his hands, trying to hide new tears.

The bombshell of his emotional announcement left a crater of silence. None dared say anything as he sat before them, obviously struggling with what he felt he had to do. Mrs. James made a feeble attempt to fill the silence.

"Oh, why didn't you say so?" Now it was time for her to feel stupid.

The discussion continued after Jack settled down some. Questions were asked, answers given. They settled on putting Jack on a bus with enough money to get there and back if things went sour. He would have to wait two weeks because he had to give a two-week notice where he had been working for the last month, Scrub 'n' Wash Car Wash. It wasn't the greatest job in the world, but he felt he had to establish some legitimate work experience. His employers told him he could have his job back if he moved back to the area.

During the two weeks, Jack continued his regular routine, which was basically helping around the house when he came home from work and spending any available time reading and studying. His enthusiasm had not faltered, but his realization of the seriousness of discipleship had grown. He also had to see if his probation would allow him to leave the state. Because he had done so well in completing his community service requirement, he received permission to leave the state. Apparently, Michigan worked out something with Georgia so he could continue his probation there. If he got in any kind of trouble, he would be sent back to Michigan for prosecution.

* * * * *

The two weeks passed quickly. Jack didn't have much to pack because he didn't own much. When he went to board his bus, he noticed it was in one of the parts of town he used to frequent. It sure looked more foreboding now than when he used to hang around the area. The enemy makes the dark things of the world seem normal, he reminded himself.

He didn't remember it from before, but the bus stopped at every little and big town along the way. Sometimes to refuel and take bathroom breaks, and other times to pick up and let off passengers. Once in a while, he would have someone sit next to him who wanted to talk, sometimes too much. One man talked the entire time about how he was from a planet in the Constellation Orion, and that he was sent to Earth to fix what was wrong. A few times, Jack told himself, he was "blessed" to have people sit next to him who didn't believe in personal hygiene. He always looked forward to when they would disembark. He ran into unusual people in his previous life, but this was a whole new kind of weird he had not seen before.

When he could, Jack spent most of the time reading and sleeping and thinking. What would he find when he got to his parents' house? He didn't dare think of it as home. He had burned that bridge long ago. He thought about Don and Becky, and how they might have changed. Surely, he had changed. He hoped they still had something in common.

Jack was still recovering from some of the physical injuries he sustained when he was savagely beaten. The bus ride didn't help. Getting in and out of the bus many times, having to switch buses, getting fitful sleep; all of this contributed to feeling like he had been beaten up again by the time he got to his hometown. He stayed at the bus station a long time, pondering whether he should take the final trip and go see his family. He was still unsure of the reception he would receive.

Jack was losing daylight when he decided to take a taxi to the house. Before he got there, he told the driver to drive by the house slowly, but not to stop. He did this several times, each time arguing with himself about whether he should just forget this and go back to Detroit. He didn't walked up his old walk that evening. Instead, he had the taxi driver drop him off at a nearby motel. He wasn't ready to meet his family yet. He would make a decision later . . . .

The next day came sooner than expected. Jack didn't sleep well again, even though he had gotten lousy sleep on the bus ride down. When he was awake during the night, he found himself praying, sometimes crying, most of the time pleading with God. He had never attempted something so difficult in his life. The physical injuries he suffered did not compare with this. He felt guilty, remorseful, ashamed, and embarrassed all at once. When he was like that, he would feel condemned, thinking of any number of things of which he was guilty. His walk with Christ had not yet reached the point where he could distinguish between the conviction of the Holy Spirit and the condemnation of the enemy.

That morning, Jack thought long and hard about what to do. He remembered how his life had changed when he became a Christian, how God had worked out his legal problems without him having to hire a lawyer. He thought about how many things had fallen in place for him since his conversion. He could not deny that God was real, and that He was watching over him. He remembered God's promise to never leave him or forsake him. Finally, he began to understand that God . . . God had his back. Whatever happened when he met his family for the first time in a long time, God was not going to cut him loose.

He checked out of the motel and started walking. Strange, most of the stores seemed closed. There wasn't much traffic on the streets, either. It was quiet enough that he could hear his feet strike the sidewalk as he walked. Then he remembered it was a holiday. That explains it, he said to himself. He rehearsed what he was going to say as he walked, and then he chuckled to himself. He reminded himself of the gangster in *The Godfather* who sat outside the office and practiced what he was going to say.

He froze as he rounded the corner to his parents' house. There was someone in the front yard. He wasn't expecting this. He didn't know what he was expecting, maybe that he would find them all together so he wouldn't have to go through four separate greetings and apologies. But life has a way of playing by its own rules. He slowly walked forward. He still had time to turn around and disappear, but his feet seemed to take on a life of their own. It seemed like a long time, but it probably wasn't very long when the person in the yard looked his way.

It was his father. He started to rehearse his line again, but before he could get two words out, his father started to run . . . to run toward him.

He wasn't expecting this, either. He froze again. He thought maybe he should run, but everything was happening so fast, he hardly had time to think. He could hear his father as he got nearer. "Jack! Jack! Jack, my boy! Jack!" His father almost threw himself on him, giving him the biggest bear hug Jack had ever experienced. Mr. Olsen stood back and looked at him momentarily, tears streaming down his cheeks. "Oh, Jack! We've missed you so bad!" Right about then, the rest of the family poured out of the house and swarmed the both of them. It was all tears and laughter and hugs and kisses right there in front of a neighbor's house down the street. Jack never got to say his prepared statement.

Jack's family was getting ready to go visit some friends when Jack showed up. That got canceled, and they all sat in the living room catching up on what had been happening with Jack and with the family. Sometimes they all talked rapid-fire at the same time. Of course, there were laughter and tears, but there were also moments of amazement at the life that Jack lived and how God had kept him safe. That was because Jack had not told them everything. He didn't tell them about almost being killed and how he came to trust God. He was waiting for the right moment to spring all that on them. If they accepted him after hearing about that part of his life, then he would know he was home.

Jack was caught up in the excitement of seeing everyone, and not being rejected outright, but as the day wore on, and they all had something to eat, he became sadder. He kept coming back to how he had let everyone down. He was contrite, but somehow his contriteness didn't match the mood in the house. His family was overjoyed to see him; he was still struggling with his failure. He was ashamed and felt unworthy of their love.

His father noticed this and addressed it first. "Son, your leaving did not change our feelings for you. Yes, we knew you would have problems, but you had a secret weapon. It was so secret that you didn't even know about it. We prayed for you every day. And God heard our prayers, as we expected. And you are here again and in your right mind."

Jack had not told them about getting beat up and losing his memory. He wondered if his father knew what he just said. Jack then proceeded to tell them the rest of the story that he had not yet shared. He didn't leave anything out. He told them about his role in dealing drugs, and how he helped build the biggest drug network in the southern part of the state. He told them about all the illegal money he made, and how he spent it chasing women. He didn't use the drugs he sold. His drug of choice was the women who were too willing to throw themselves at him because of the power and money he had. He told them about how he had the power of life and death over people, although he never used that power. And he told them about how he almost died when he got beat up, how he spent a long time in the hospital ICU, and later in a regular room, trying to regain his memory and heal from the many broken bones and wounds he suffered. He told them how he had been at risk for going to prison for a murder he didn't know if he had taken part in or not. His parents, Becky, and even Don were crying at his telling the gruesome details of his last few years.

Then he told them how he came to Christ, how he instantly recovered his memory, and how his legal problems were solved through his probation and community service. Finally, Jack said he would understand if his family did not want to have anything to do with him. He was sorry, but he knew that being sorry was not going to undo all the evil he had been a part of. At this point, his dad stopped him. He had heard enough.

"Son, what you did in the past is terrible. But you don't live in the past. You live in the present. And the God of the past and the present is also the God of the future. You have put yourself in His hands, under His Lordship, and that is more than good enough.

"Let me be clear. You have never ceased being my son. My love for you is not dependent on what you do. I love you because I choose to love you. I love you enough to give my life for you. I wish I had taken the beating you took. You don't earn that kind of love. You receive it as a gift."

Jack could not believe his ears. He had spent countless hours worried about how he was going to be received. He was pretty sure his parents would reject him outright. He knew he had messed up enough to be disowned. No one would hold it against his parents if they kicked him out right then and there. Instead, Jack experienced a love that he did not deserve and could never earn. For the first time, he had an inkling of what grace truly means. He knew that mercy has to do with not receiving what you deserve. Now he understood that grace has to do with getting what you don't deserve. His father had extended grace to him. He would never forget.

Don and Becky witnessed Jack's return to the family; both were amazed at their father's reaction. They expected their mother to be a bucket of tears, but they expected their father to be much more judgmental. Instead, he received Jack back with what appeared to be unconditional love. They had never seen this before. For Don, especially, it caused him to pause and think about his own feelings about Jack since he left. Although he didn't really want it to happen, he had allowed an attitude of bitterness to take root in his heart toward Jack. He could feel anger rising up in him when he saw his mother quietly crying. Dad was a little harder to read, but Don knew he had to be having similar feelings, especially when he saw his wife struggling. Dad himself couldn't be immune to the hurt. After all, Jack was his firstborn. He was the proverbial guinea pig on which Dad could practice all the parenting philosophies he thought he knew. Dad and Mom would sometimes laugh at how ignorant they were when it came to raising kids, and they prayed a lot that Jack would survive their mistakes. Jack was born at a time when cloth diapers were still being used. Mom would tell the story of the time she changed his diaper and accidentally pinned one side to his skin! Of course, little Jack cried, and when she realized what she had done, she cried. There were other parenting bloopers, some having to do with Don and Becky. If they happened today, they might have had their kids taken away from them. They were now funny stories they told on each other during the holidays or family reunions.

Becky had also struggled with Jack's absence. She didn't like the way he dealt with Susan. As young as she was at the time, she sometimes imagined Susan getting married to Jack and becoming her sister-in-law. That would be perfect, she thought. But Jack broke Susan's heart, and Becky held a grudge against him for it. This was one of those unintended effects Jack did not know about when he was making plans to leave home. In her mind, again and again, Becky went over what she would tell Jack when she got the chance. In her own way, she was planning to give him a piece of her mind. They had never discussed it, but Don had been thinking the same thing for different reasons.

That all changed when they saw their parents' reaction to Jack coming home. If anyone had reason to be angry at Jack, it was their parents. Don and Becky had seen how they were affected by his absence. Mom threw herself into extra activities at church and school, beyond the normal activities that they used to do to support Don and Becky. After a while, she withdrew into herself; she seemed to smile less and less. Dad did a similar thing, throwing himself into his work. He also took Mom out on dates more, but that began to dwindle as well, as he too began to withdraw into himself. The only thing that kept them steady and involved was that they still had Don and Becky at home. They still wanted to show them their love and support, no less so than what they had done for Jack.

Instead of confronting Jack, Don and Becky accepted him back, as their parents did. They were in the room when Dad told Jack he didn't have to earn his love. They heard him say he would always be their son. They assumed what he said to Jack applied to them as well. That was an unexpected blessing, and it brought great relief to them. Neither they nor their parents knew they had a need for such reassurance, but it had its effect anyway.

Mom and Dad's joy overflowed. They each called and told their friends about Jack coming home. Don and Becky got to hear them tell the story over and over. They replayed the event each time, and Mom, especially, got emotional each time she told the story. Don and Becky did some of the same. Don told his friends at school who knew Jack. Becky told her friends at school, too, and she made sure to tell Susan. Susan had already heard about it from her parents, but she and Becky rejoiced together anyway.

* * * * *

In the meantime, Jack set out to try and establish himself. He began a new job, but not at his father's business. He didn't want special treatment, and he wanted to prove himself by starting at the bottom. He got a job as a parts runner at a local Kia dealership. This was perfect for him. He knew almost nothing about cars. He got to drive around part of the day picking up parts at other area dealerships, and when he wasn't doing that work, he swept floors, cleaned bathrooms, and drove customers to their homes in the courtesy van. He learned about the car business and how to serve and interact with all kinds of people. In time, he got a chance to sell cars, and his income went up. He knew how to sell, but he insisted on being the most honest salesman on the lot. God honored his honesty and prospered him.

Jack kept his practice of Bible study and prayer. He joined his family at the church they attended since he was a child. Some of the people knew a little about his story. He got involved more than he ever had before, but he soon learned that there are only so many hours in the day. He had to balance his time requirements. There would always be more work to do than the time to do it all. All this time working, studying, and volunteering at church prevented him from much of a social life. He looked at his time in church as his social life, so he wasn't as disappointed as some might think. When asked if he had a girlfriend, he would just smile. He decided that if God wanted him to have a girlfriend, He would send him one without Jack getting too worked up about it.

That didn't keep people from trying to set him up with their friends or cousins or daughters or nieces or "just the perfect girl" for him. He would be invited to some social gathering, and wouldn't you know it? There would be all couples there except for Jack and one other young woman. A few times, he was invited to dinner at people's houses. When he got there, there would be two or three older couples, and a young single woman about his age. All of these experiences made Jack feel like he was being interviewed for a job. It gave a new meaning to "awkward" as far as he was concerned. He wasn't sure if some of the women felt the same way.

*****

"Susan is in town visiting her parents for the weekend." Jack wasn't sure why Becky told him that piece of information, but he felt a tinge of appreciation having heard it.

"OK. And that means what?" He didn't want to give any impression that he was glad to hear the news.

"For one thing, it means we get to hang out," Becky said. "I don't see her very much since she went off to college and works a part-time job. It might also give you a chance to say hi to each other."

Jack had made things right with everyone he could find. Only two remained on the list, and one of them was Susan. It wasn't that he didn't want to talk with her. He just didn't know what he would say. It was beginning to look like he was going to have to talk to her whether he was ready or not. As he thought about it, it might not matter that he didn't know what he would say. His history with preplanned statements was not very good! Every time he went to say one of his well-rehearsed lines, he would fumble around and say something completely different. It seemed like his words were being directed from somewhere else.

Jack didn't see Susan until Sunday at church. Even then, they exchanged only a brief greeting. Like most Sundays, Jack was busy helping out where he could. He had been made a deacon a while back, and there didn't seem to be much down time at this large church he attended. And one other thing happened that morning that embarrassed Jack a bit. One of the older ladies brought her adult granddaughter by to meet him. He knew the script by now. He would shake hands and express appreciation for their having met, make some small talk, and find an excuse to move on. This wasn't hard since there was plenty to do. He didn't know if Susan saw this meeting or not. Part of him hoped she did.

*****

Jack enjoyed his sales job at the dealership more than he thought he would. He was making enough money that he would soon be able to move into his own apartment, and if he kept it up, he would even be able to afford a used car. They provided a car for him at his job, but it wasn't his to keep; he really wanted one of his own. He was also learning about running a business. He always made time in the week to sit with the finance woman and learn how she did her job. Then, at other times, he would have long conversations with his father about his business. He was comparing and contrasting the approaches of the two companies, and he was learning a lot. He didn't know if anyone else learned this way. He actually picked up this way of learning when he was comparing and contrasting religions. Some skills are transferable, and he appreciated that he had learned some useful ones in his short life.

* * * * *

On a Thursday a few weeks later, as they were sitting around the dinner table, Becky's eyes got wide, and she exclaimed, "Oh no! I gotta get something!" She ran from the table and searched until she found her phone. When she found it, she hurried back to the table and furiously looked through her email messages. "Where is it? Where is it!?" Whatever she was looking for, she couldn't find it. She switched to her contacts. Whatever it was, it was important to her. "C'mon, c'mon, where is it? There! There it is!"

"What is so important?" Jack was laughing at the way Becky had jumped up from the table and searched for her phone.

"Here! I'm sorry. I forgot. Susan told me to give you her contact information if you wanted it. I'm so sorry. I got busy and forgot." Becky was making more out of this than it was. Besides, Jack didn't know if he was going to contact Susan or not.

"Don't worry about it. The world won't end if you forget to give me a number," Jack said. He suspected that Becky was hoping that they would get back together, and fearing that she had almost messed up the chance of that ever happening. He didn't think it was ever going to happen anyway because, for one, he wasn't interested, and two, Susan probably wasn't either. What he was struggling with was how he was going to make things right with her after he left the way he did three years earlier.

He had a few other people on the list with whom he had to make things right. Two of them were Margaret and Miriam. It wasn't that he did anything wrong, but he had to thank them for the influence they had on him regarding his faith. He had acted like he didn't care or had better things to do, but he heard them when they spoke about Christ and watched them as they lived their new faith. There was a positive impact that he was not aware of until later when he had a chance to look back on the "divine appointments" that he experienced on his way to salvation. He wrote them a nice handwritten letter which he rewrote many times because he wanted to say what he felt in just the right words. Then he wrote an identical copy and mailed it to their separate addresses. They would be surprised to hear from him this way since they were not used to writing or receiving letters. And yes, he would later hear from them that they were surprised and glad to hear from him, and that they were glad that he came to know Christ like they did. They were doing fine and growing in their faith. They also told him that each of them framed his letter to encourage themselves when they needed it. He smiled when he received their response. He wasn't expecting that.

The last person he had to seek out was Mr. Simpson. This was going to be different. In this situation, he would have to eat crow. Mr. Simpson gave him good counsel nearly four years ago, and because of his hard-heartedness, Jack rejected it. If he had paid attention, he could have avoided a lot of pain, emotionally and physically. So Jack decided he would take some time off work and show up at Mr. Simpson's office unexpectedly one mid-morning. It was a fleece before God. If Mr. Simpson was not there, he would take it as a sign that God didn't expect him to speak with him. He hoped that was the case. Jack was, quite frankly, tired of being embarrassed. As he stood at the doorway, God must have been smiling. A familiar voice started speaking as a man walked up behind him.

"Is that Jack Olsen? Is that you, Jack? Well, I'll be. Come on in my office with me. I just got done with a meeting, and I have the rest of the day free." Jack felt like he had chains on his feet as Mr. Simpson practically bounced into his office.

"Sit down. Sit down. Wow, it's been a long time. Catch me up. How's the family? What have you been up to?"

Jack was still amazed at how God had answered his fleece. The rest of the day free? It might take that long for Jack to tell what had happened in the last three years.

Mr. Simpson sensed Jack pause. "Would you like something to drink? I've got some juice in the fridge, or I could make some coffee if you like." Mr. Simpson saw that Jack was uncomfortable, and he was trying to make it easy on him. "You know, I thought about you a lot these last three years," he went on. "I saw your family at church and would ask them about you, but apparently you cut them off. What was that all about? Then I heard you were back, but I was beginning to doubt it because I thought I would see you in church, if anywhere, and I didn't."

Jack didn't want to tell Mr. Simpson that he had been avoiding him, but he had. He was trying to get up the courage to come see him. He accepted his offer of some juice, took a sip, and began to talk.

"Well, you're right so far. I did cut my family off because I wanted to make it on my own. I did return some months ago. I intentionally avoided you at church because I wasn't ready to see you yet. I'm ready now." Jack inherited his directness from his father's side of the family. More often than not, he used it wisely.

"I came today to eat some crow. I may leave here very fat from all the crow I have to eat."

Mr. Simpson let him talk. Jack used his skills of observation to see how he was being received. So far, it seemed to be going all right.

Jack went on and told Mr. Simpson what happened after he last talked with him. He told about getting to Detroit only to find he didn't have a job waiting—and no apartment either. He had to move in with his friend's family. He told him about getting involved in a life of crime, and how he almost ended up in jail for murder. Finally, he told about his near death beating, and how he found faith in Christ, and how his life had changed. Jack realized now that he had been blinded by his own greed and ignorance the last time he spoke with Mr. Simpson. He now agreed with what Mr. Simpson said back then, that his father was really looking out for him when he resisted his leaving to go out on his own. Jack talked a lot, and Mr. Simpson listened, with few interruptions. The time flew, and before they knew it, it was past lunchtime.

"Jack, I'm glad you learned your lesson. By all accounts, since you returned, you've made a very good impression on folks. I think you ought to consider telling an abbreviated form of your story at church sometime. You have had so many experiences of God helping you that people cannot help but be in awe of God working. It might help them get through some of what they are going through too. And have you thought about going to college?"

"Yes, I have, but I have to work some more before I'll be ready," Jack said. "I'm thinking of looking into it for the second semester next year, and maybe taking a few online classes before then."

"Well, you know that I'm here to help if you need me. I know a thing or two about higher education." Mr. Simpson smiled, hoping Jack would remember that he had counseled him to go to college way back when. Jack smiled back. He caught the message.

Their visit ended with Jack promising to see Mr. Simpson again, and promising not to avoid him at church.

Jack had enough time to go back and work a few hours at his job. He had to figure out how to finish his list.

FOURTEEN

No Greater Love

Like Becky forgetting to get Susan's contact information to Jack, he forgot to call Susan for a while. Actually, he probably forgot on purpose because he still didn't know what he was going to say. He finally got up the courage to begin the conversation by texting her. He figured that was the least threatening approach. If she wanted to talk more, she would acknowledge his message. If not, he would understand.

> Hi Susan. Sorry we didn't get to talk much when you were in the area a couple of weeks ago.

Susan saw the text right away. She decided to wait a couple of days before responding. She didn't want to give the impression that she was desperate to talk to Jack because she wasn't. Sure, she was curious, but that was different.

She lasted a day.

> Hi Jack. Got your message. How's it going?

It took her thirty minutes, at least, to create that response. The two of them continued texting, and each would always wait a day before responding. They continued this dance until they agreed to meet for coffee the next time she was in town. There wasn't a long weekend coming up, so Susan would only be in town for two days the next time she visited her parents, and she usually spent some of that time with Becky. She would have to carve out some time for Jack and hope Becky didn't ask too many questions.

Jack kept himself busy enough that he didn't have much time to think about Susan. He was basically in a holding mode. He expected that she would text him when she decided to visit. Susan was busy as well. She had one more year before she graduated, and time was flying by fast. She had to decide if she was going to apply for medical school or work full-time. Her part-time job had flexible hours, but she still had only twenty-four hours in a day.

When they finally met, it was at a French bakery that they used to frequent when Susan lived in town. It was well known for its pastries and coffee. They met right after lunch. The place was relatively empty, so they were able to talk without the noise of the lunch crowd drowning them out.

"Wow, it's been a while since I've been here," Susan said, and she no doubt approved of Jack's choice. She was at ease, and that helped put Jack at ease.

"Yeah, me too," Jack said. "Lots of good memories from back then. I remember a lot of good times associated with this place."

Susan asked Jack if he told Becky about their meeting. He said he planned to ask Susan the same thing! Both just wanted to get together without having to answer Becky's probing questions. They laughed at the sneakiness of it all. There was a lot of catching up and laughter and reminiscing. After what seemed like a few minutes, they looked at the clock, and it was late afternoon. Time had gotten away from them. Somewhere in the several hours of too much coffee and pastries, Jack was able to apologize for the way he left her hanging when he moved. She graciously accepted his apology and said something about them being younger at the time and not really knowing what to do. Jack didn't know how Susan felt, but he felt relieved that she was still talking to him. Both of them knew they had changed a lot since those days, and there were no illusions about getting back together. They would be friends, good friends, for now.

They left the bakery laughing about how Jack was going to handle Becky's inquisitiveness. Even though Becky didn't know they were going to meet, she was no dummy. With both of them in town, she suspected they would find time to get together. It would make sense for them to see each other since she knew Jack wanted to apologize for being stupid. Susan would not have to deal with Becky until the next day at church.

* * * * *

Jack saved enough money to get his own apartment. Before too much longer, he had his own car. He was a full-blown independent and responsible adult. He had the best of both worlds. He was making his way in life, and his parents were still close by for him to visit. It was a win-win for everyone. On top of that, he was taking college classes at night. There had been some talk at church about Jack possibly going into the ministry, and he was willing to do it if it was God's will for his life. He had no problem giving up his own ambitions in that regard. He wanted to be faithful to what was often called the Great Commission. Maybe he was supposed to be a pastor. But the more he prayed and studied his Bible, the more he became convinced that the Great Commission applied to all believers. It was the responsibility of every believer to share their faith. It wasn't just for pastors or preachers.

Jack grew steadily in his faith. He learned to discern when the Holy Spirit was talking, and when he was just imagining things. There were a few times he avoided trouble by turning right at the Spirit's prompting instead of going left, as he wanted. There was one drawback in maturing in his Christian walk. Other believers started to fall to the side. It wasn't that they didn't love Jesus. It seemed they did. It was just that they refused to put in the effort to grow closer to Him. Discipleship meant something different to some of these other believers, maybe just attending a bunch of church activities, in some cases. To Jack, it seemed that their faith was an addendum to their lives; for him, it was everything. He found himself having less in common with some of the people in his own church. He would want to talk about kingdom life; they would want to talk about football. He would want to talk about serving; they would want to talk about the latest thing on social media. He knew it wasn't wrong to have other interests, but it seemed like Jesus was an afterthought, and not a priority, for many.

Meanwhile, Susan and Jack became better friends than they ever were as boyfriend and girlfriend. She decided to apply to medical school, and that was taking up much of her time, as if she had a lot of extra time to begin with. The biggest loser was Becky. Whenever Susan came to visit, Becky had to share their time with Jack.

All in all, everyone was getting along. Susan's family was good friends with Jack's family. In fact, sometimes it seemed like they were all related to each other. Susan's father liked the new and improved Jack. He was still a bit of a helicopter dad, but he trusted Jack to be responsible and a gentleman with his daughter. Don was back to looking up to his big brother. He learned from Jack's negative experiences, and from his turning to Christ. Dad told him once that he would make enough mistakes on his own, so it was better to learn from other people's mistakes than to make the same ones yourself.

* * * * *

"Jack, can we meet at the French place when I come to visit this weekend?" Susan sounded almost giddy.

"Sure. I'm always up for the bakery. Any special reason?" Jack had noticed her different tone, but he didn't know what, if anything, it could mean. Probably nothing. Susan had not been to visit her parents in a while, and she was probably excited about spending time at home and seeing old friends. She was due a break from her heavy academic load and her work.

They had been to the bakery enough that they discovered there was a lull in business from around 10 a.m. until 11:30 a.m., and then the lunch crowd would start pouring in. It worked out well for them because they could spend a decent time talking, be out before the lunch rush, and each still have time to do other things during the afternoon.

This particular day it had rained the night before, and the weather was a bit foggy, even misty, in the morning. Most of that had evaporated by the time they met at the bakery, but it was still cloudy and somewhat gray. It was supposed to clear up by afternoon. They figured they were in the right place at the right time. This time, Susan chose the pastry. They always took turns choosing the pastry, which they then shared because it was always too big for one of them. Coffees and half-pastry in hand, they sat down at their favorite spot. By this time, Jack could tell something was up, but he waited for Susan to tell him.

He didn't have to wait long. Even before they sat down, she looked like a child who had just received her favorite gift for Christmas.

"I got accepted to medical school. There! I said it! I've known for over a week, but I didn't want to tell anyone until I told you in person." Before he could say anything, she was jumping up and down and giving Jack a big hug.

"Congratulations! I'm so happy for you!" He hugged her back and joined her in a sort of jumping-up-and-down-thing next to the table.

"I knew you could do it. You were always the smart one. You say you haven't told anyone else? Not even your parents?"

"That's right. I didn't want for you to hear it from someone else by accident."

"Well, I feel honored. For the first time, I know something about you first that Becky doesn't know." They laughed, and sat down with Jack facing the window. He noticed that the pavement was drying up and the sun breaking through. Jack would ask a few questions, and Susan would talk a mile a minute, telling him what would happen next, what school she was accepted to, how much it cost, how she planned to pay for it, and more. Of course, this would require many adjustments, but she was up to the challenge.

They both decided to go to the restroom on the way out. They agreed to meet right after so Jack could walk her to her car. Susan had to wait for someone to finish in the women's room, so Jack got a head start. While he was finishing up, he heard a commotion outside. He figured it was probably a worker dropping some trays. He would hate to have to be the one to clean up such a mess.

There were still some muffled noises Jack could hear as he washed his hands. When he finished, he walked out of the restroom and saw the commotion. There was an apparently angry customer yelling at the cashier. Everyone else was standing back, as if to see how this would play out. *Where's Susan?*, Jack wondered.

Then he saw it. The guy had a gun and was pointing it at the cashier. He wasn't a disgruntled customer. He was robbing the place. And he wasn't just yelling at the cashier. He was threatening everyone, yelling that he would shoot if anyone made a move. Jack knew enough about drug users to know that this guy was high, desperate, and unpredictable.

"Look, man, you don't have to do this," Jack offered. "I can get you some help."

"Shut up!" He was surprised by Jack. His head jerked toward him in such a way that if two or three people had rushed him, they probably would have been able to subdue him. Jack couldn't blame anyone for not doing anything. Probably, none of them were trained.

"Look, there's not much money here," Jack said softly but firmly. "The lunch rush hasn't started yet. Let me help you, man. You don't want to do this."

"I told you to shut up! Another word out of you, and I'll shoot you first! That goes for everyone else, too!" The robber turned his attention back to the cashier, who had not moved an inch. The man began to wave his gun carelessly in all directions. His behavior was getting more erratic by the second.

Jack was still looking for Susan when she stepped from the ladies restroom. She was not aware anything was happening until she saw a guy pointing a gun in her direction. Jack saw it at the same time. He had seen that look before. As if by instinct, Jack lunged to place himself between Susan and the shooter before . . . the sound of the gun going off echoed throughout the bakery.

Susan screamed.

EPILOGUE

Jack Olsen's memorial service took place in his home church. Extra chairs were brought out to accommodate the overflow crowd. You would have thought a celebrity was there to hold a concert. The pastor looked out over the people and, veering from the program, asked anyone who had been won to Christ by Jack's words or example to stand. Hundreds responded.

This was truly a going home celebration. Many told stories of their lives with Jack. Some were sad, some were funny. All revealed inspiring facets of Jack's impact on people from all walks of life.

Jack was young when he died. Some would be tempted to be angry at God because Jack hadn't lived a full life. Or had he? He probably lived and did more in his short life than many who die much older.

Those who know about these things would say that Jack didn't really start living until he had established a relationship with God through Jesus Christ. He was forgiven much, and he loved much. The rest of his life was spent trying to live up to the greatest commandments: "Love the Lord your God with all your heart and with all your soul and with all your mind and with all your strength. And love your neighbor as yourself."

Love was the key. The love of God for Jack, and his love for God and others, was what motivated him. And in the end, when he saved Susan's life by placing himself in the path of a crazed man's bullet, his way up ended at the peak of love.

"Greater love has no one than this: to lay down one's life for one's friends."